Leona B. Slru

P9-DEZ-927

The Brittle Thread

The Brittle Thread

by Douglas Hall

ZONDERVAN PUBLISHING HOUSE
GRAND RAPIDS   MICHIGAN

THE BRITTLE THREAD
Copyright (c) 1968 by Zondervan Publishing House, Grand Rapids, Mich.

Library of Congress Catalog Card Number 68-57430

All rights reserved. No portion of this book may be reproduced in any way, without the written permission of the publishers, except for brief excerpts in magazine reviews, etc.

PRINTED IN THE UNITED STATES OF AMERICA

To
Joyce

Foreword

Douglas Hall is a man who moves—fast, straight and with intense purpose. He is a dynamo of energy—one of those eighteen-hour-a-day people whose major problem is the rest of us who lag behind at a pace that might pass the tortoise but never overtake the hare.

He is an intellectual—not in that stodgy sense that cloisters a man within library walls, nor in that irritating sense that makes a "thing" out of it. But Douglas Hall is a thinker with a mind that is clean, cutting, knowledgeable and overflowing with ideas. He manages to turn his information into action—the sort of action that moves people and does things.

Douglas Hall had the advantage of being born in a predominantly Christian country, reared in a home which maintained a constant Christian emphasis and belonging to a Christian Church such as The Peoples Church. He has successfully interwoven his background and beliefs into his work in a remarkable way not usually found in this style of writing.

The Brittle Thread moves. It is fast. It reaches out and "grabs" you in the first sentence and doesn't let go until the last.

The Brittle Thread is realistic. The characters are believable and very much alive. They are the kind of people that walk down our streets, work in our offices and live in our homes. The plot is not mere fantasy, it does what every good story should do—it carries the reader out of his own immediate world and opens the door to another realm of activity.

The Brittle Thread has a Christian thrust. It is not a "souped-up" sentimental orgy that makes everybody good and everything turn out nice. It doesn't sermonize. It is pure fiction written to entertain people who are fed up with the blood-and-guts, sex-for-sex'-sake, girls-and-boys-and-beds-unlimited that have become the accepted format of the average modern novel.

The Brittle Thread should be read and re-read and in the years that are ahead a person may be grateful to God for the work of Douglas Hall.

PAUL B. SMITH
Minister, The Peoples Church

Toronto, Canada

The Brittle Thread

Chapter 1

THE HUMIDITY INDEX was well past 86%; it was hot, sticky and extremely uncomfortable. The heat hung low like a smothering blanket, covering everything within reach, including the slumped figure in the corner of the chesterfield.

Beads of perspiration stood out on the man's forehead and dark patches of sweat blotched the front of his shirt and around the arms.

In the distance, a whirring fan could be heard, broken only by the labored breathing and occasional rasping cough of the man.

On a coffee table, directly in front of the chesterfield, was a pencil and crumpled piece of paper. The writing became increasingly illegible as it tapered off into a scrawl half way down the page.

In the dimly lit room the man stirred, attempted to stand up, only to lose his balance and fall, arms flailing, to the floor, upsetting the coffee table and spewing the cluttered mess ahead of his falling body. Just beyond his outstretched hand was an empty bottle with the label, "only to be taken on the advice of a physician," staring up from the carpet.

In the foggy unreality of semi-consciousness Jimmy Ferguson tried to collect his thoughts. It seemed like a lifetime, but he knew it could only have been a few hours at the very most since he decided to take matters into his own hands. Up to then he had been content to let the others find some way out of the mess, but all that quickly changed with the telephone call. He knew at the time he should have waited for Brainerd and Potter. It was stupid of him to play the hero.

Somewhere off in the mist of reality muffled voices and thudding feet came through.

"Jimmy, Jimmy, where are you?"

It sounded like Betty's voice, but how could it be? How could she know where he was? Who told her?

In the hall, three people with desperate looks on their faces rapidly converged on the door at the end of the hall.

"He must be in here, we've checked all the other rooms," said the older man between gasps for breath.

"Jimmy, it's Betty, are you in there?"

"Take it easy, Betty, let me try."

With a gentle sweep of his arm the younger man moved the girl aside and rapped on the door, "Jim, it's me, Paul Brainerd, open the door."

Ferguson tried to pull himself up on one arm, but he just collapsed, making an ominous thud on the floor.

"Did you hear that? Someone's in there," said the girl, her voice on the verge of breaking.

"What's going on here, are you trying to waken the whole rooming house?"

The speaker was a rumpled woman in a dressing gown far too small for her ample figure.

No one answered, both the men and the woman were pressing their heads to the panel of the door, trying to hear.

A strong arm pulled Brainerd away. "What's going on here, can't anyone answer a civil question? I've a good mind to call the police."

"I wish you would, madam. We're going to need one," he replied without taking his ear away from the door.

A number of people in various degrees of undress gathered in the hall, watching the drama as it unfolded. Occasionally one would make an aside, but for the most part they said nothing, just watched.

"Listen, I own this place and if you don't tell me what you're up

2

to I'm going to raise the roof. I could have you all arrested for trespassing, I know the law."

"Lady, for the last time please call the police," Brainerd's voice was becoming increasingly exasperated. "I'm going to break this door down."

"You're what? Why do you want to do a thing like that?"

"There's a man in there probably dying—is that a good enough reason for you?"

"You can't come in here and wreck my place, I won't stand for it."

"Watch me." With that Brainerd took a few steps back and hunching his shoulder low took a run at the door. The wood, obviously old, splintered easily, but the door still hung on by one hinge and the night chain.

As Brainerd gathered himself for another assault the landlady turned abruptly around and pushed her way through the collection of people, muttering to herself about what she was going to do when the police arrived.

"Once more should do it." Brainerd took another run at the panel; this time it gave and he went flying into the room closely followed by his two companions.

In the gloom they saw a sprawled figure on the floor and Betty immediately fell to her knees and cradled the limp head in her lap with tears streaming down her face.

"It's Betty, darling, everything is going to be all right now," she whispered in his ear.

Brainerd flicked on the light switch and turned to look at the straining faces which filled the empty doorway.

"It's all right, you can go back to your rooms. Sorry to have disturbed you," he said as he picked up the shattered door and leaned the largest remaining piece against the wall.

From the hallway came a shrill, agitated voice, "They just told me to get out of my own house, can you imagine that, officer? My own house. Not only that, they broke a door down. Who's going to pay for the damage? I want you to arrest them, all three of them. I run a respectable boarding house. I. . . ."

"Yes, Mrs. Munroe, we know, now take it easy until we see what's happened," said the officer as he cut her off in mid-sentence.

"Move aside please, move aside," he ordered pushing his way into the room.

"You got here fast," said the older man.

"We were just passing in front when Mrs. Munroe called us. Now what's going on here?"

"This man's dying from an overdose of sleeping pills, can you call for an ambulance?" asked Brainerd.

The officer knelt beside the man and felt his pulse. "It looks like an overdose all right. Bill, here's the bottle. I'll call."

"All right, hurry back."

The officer stepped out into the hall, "Go back to your rooms, we'll be in touch if we want to talk to any of you. Where's the nearest telephone?"

"You can use mine, officer," said a small grayhaired woman in a worn dressing gown. "Isn't it awful? I just knew that young man was headed for grief when I saw him this afternoon, I just knew it."

The officer followed the woman down the hall and into a cluttered bed-sitting room. "You saw him this afternoon?"

"Yes."

"What time?"

"About two-thirty."

The officer reached for the phone and began dialing.

Back in the room the other policeman had his note book out and was beginning to ask questions.

"May I have your name?" he asked pointing to the older man.

"Harrison Phinnamore, Reverend Harrison Phinnamore."

"And you?"

"Paul Brainerd."

"Miss?"

The girl looked up from the floor, her eyes puffy and red, "Betty Ferguson."

4

"Who's our friend?" he asked, pointing to the figure on the floor with his pencil.

"James Ferguson," answered Phinnamore. "He's my assistant."

Before the questioning could go any further the other officer called from the doorway, "Bill, can I see you for a moment?"

"Excuse me."

The two men talked in hushed whispers, occasionally looking at the two men in the room and the girl on the floor.

"The ambulance will be here in a moment. Could you please come down to the station? We'll need a statement from each one of you."

"I want to go with Jimmy. Don't let them take him away from me," sobbed the girl.

"Can't she go to the hospital with him, officer?" asked Brainerd.

"Can't see why not, we can get her statement later. I'll speak to the ambulance attendant."

"Here they are now, Bill."

Two men in white jackets came into the room with a stretcher and quickly bundled Ferguson on it and adjusted the straps.

As they were wheeling him out Brainerd touched the officer's arm, "I'm afraid I didn't catch your name, officer."

"Sorry, I'm P. C. Bill Jenkins and my partner is P. C. Harry Jones. Say, you look familiar. I'm sure we've met before."

"Don't think so—I've only been in town for a couple of weeks."

The ambulance roared down the nearly deserted street, with the revolving light on its roof casting eerie red fingers on the parked cars. As it wheeled into the main thoroughfare its siren cut through the noise of traffic like a vengeful marauder.

"He'll be all right, won't he?" asked Betty as she looked up into the face of the young intern.

"We'll know in a few moments. It's not much further to the hospital."

Ferguson started to cough. The involuntary movement stirred his subconscious and he fought to orient himself once again.

Where was he, what was happening? He tried to open his eyes, but the effort was too great. Somewhere he thought he could **hear a** telephone ringing. Why didn't someone answer it?

The telephone, that's what started it, that's when everything began. If only he had let it ring and had never answered it . . . .

He knew that someone was lifting him but didn't care. He was trying to remember what had happened.

Chapter 2

FAIRVIEW COMMUNITY CHURCH was a staid, well-respected house of worship in the community. Its minister, the Reverend Harrison Phinnamore, was also staid and well-respected.

Like his church, which had not welcomed one new member in the past eighteen months, Phinnamore had become infected with a lack of enthusiasm and drive.

In his younger years he had been dynamic and exciting. His ministry was the talk of the entire area and by implementing imaginative methods of sermon presentation he had filled his church night after night. This was all history. His sermons had taken on a tired, "I won't bother them, if they'll not bother me" attitude.

His lack of enthusiasm contaminated the congregation which slowly dwindled. The young married couples began leaving for other churches and the young people just stayed away, not even responding to one or two attempts by the minister to plan something out of the ordinary for a Sunday evening service.

The indifference of the spiritual and physical condition of the congregation troubled a number on the church board. This group of elected men had the responsibility for the administrative work of the church. They met monthly and it had become a foregone conclusion that it would be a short meeting. All Phinnamore usually did was make a couple of requests for new hymn books or additional literature for the tract rack in the church foyer. Outside of some innocuous remarks his only other contribution was the benediction at the closing of the meeting.

The unrest was growing and came to a head two days before a

scheduled monthly meeting. Dick Hart, chairman of the evangelism committee, felt that unless something was done, and done quickly, Fairview stood in the very great danger of just fading away. Probably, he said, within a year or so Fairview might actually be forced to close its doors because of its poor spiritual condition and lack of identification with the community.

Hart felt so strongly about the matter that he decided to do something about it instead of just sitting back and letting the inevitable happen. Realizing that unless he used discretion and moved carefully the situation could quickly get out of hand, he tried to make sure of anyone he spoke to about the problem. Having once come through a church split he had no intention of being a party to such an unsavory situation again. However, he felt a responsibility to his fellow members and vowed to try everything within his power to get Fairview back to the position of influence it once enjoyed. It was a great source of embarrassment to him personally whenever he had to justify or defend his membership. People constantly asked what had happened to Fairview.

His campaign started with a survey of the congregation. This he did with the help of his older son Mark. For a four week period they counted the congregation, broke it down into age groups and plotted the results on a large chart hung on the wall of his den at home. Being an active member of the general council he had no trouble getting access to the church records.

For a number of evenings he and Mark looked up the history of the church and plotted the past attendance, which was kept for statistical purposes over the years. In addition to attendance records Hart also graphed the current giving against the past, plus the missionary program which had fallen off to the point of being almost nonexistent.

Armed with this material he approached five other members of the council and asked them to come to his house for a private meeting.

According to the by-laws of the church all that was needed to present a motion to the council was a quorum, and with fourteen men on the council Hart only needed four or more to support his brief.

As is the case with all revolutionaries he hand-picked his supporters and as also is the case, with those involved with change, he rationalized his actions. He was confident he was right.

The meeting was long and stormy. Four of those invited saw the logic in his argument, but one man, Charlie Scales, erupted into a torrent of abuse and stormed out of the house. He would have no part of censuring Phinnamore, a man who he said was an inspiration and had his wholehearted support. His abrupt departure left the remaining gathering unnerved and indecisive.

It took nearly an hour of serious talking before Hart felt he had regained the confidence of the men. Once the tone of the meeting had settled down he gave each one of them a mimeographed piece of paper. It was headed, "Motion Re Spiritual Condition of Fairview Community Church."

As each one read the document there was an uneasy silence except for the asthmatic wheezing of Harry Boland, a large muscular man who, despite his robust appearance was really physically unwell.

"Boy, you really laid it on the line," said Alan Hayes.

"Can you think of a better way to bring this situation to a head?" replied Hart.

"I'm not complaining, just pointing out that we're doing the right thing. After all there's a man's future at stake."

"What do the rest of you think?" asked Hart as he looked around the room searching each face for some indication of acceptance or rejection.

Following a prolonged silence he turned to Steve Gordon, "You haven't said a thing since we started—what's your opinion, Steve?"

Gordon was a small, fair-haired man, deadly serious at all times and completely lacking any sense of humor. "I want more time to think this over. I agree in principle, something has to be done. I wish there was some other way."

"Wait a moment all of you." The speaker was Alton J. Brent, the only man left who had not expressed an opinion. "I have been sitting here for most of the night listening to the arguments for and against what's being proposed. I didn't say anything when Charlie walked out. Frankly, for a moment I was tempted to join him. After hearing each one of you I'm not so sure but that I made a mistake by not leaving with him."

"There's the door, Alt. If that's what you think, you'd better get going," snapped Boland.

"Hold it, Harry, give him a chance," said Hart.

"Chance, we've listened to him for years and where has it gotten us?"

"What do you mean by that crack?" demanded Brent.

"Forget it, it was nothing."

"No, I won't forget it, before I continue with this lunacy I want the air cleared up."

"All right I'll tell you what's bothering me, it's you. Ever since you joined our church you have tried to lead everyone around by the nose including Phinnamore. You've always been outspoken and said what you thought and personally I don't understand why you ever came tonight, especially in view of your apparent friendship with the pastor."

The other men leaned forward in their chairs, eyes riveted on the two men. This was one of the few times that Alton Brent's position in the church had ever been challenged openly and they smelled the kill.

Brent sat back massaging his chin with one hand. Hart opened his mouth to speak, but was silenced by Brent's raised hand. "Well now, what have we here? I take it that you don't like m.y approach to the things of God. Well, let me tell you something, all of you. I run a successful business, a very successful business in fact, and, if my authority was challenged by a group of amateurs such as yourselves I'd fire the lot and laugh as you were thrown out of my office. What do you think you're playing at, Sunday school? I'll tell you what you're playing at, it could be the destruction of a man's life. His entire past and future is in your hands and all you can do is say you're not sure. What are you trying to achieve? The runination of a man or the building up of work? Up to now everything has been negative. You've listed the things that haven't been done instead of concentrating on the things that have. If you want my opinion your little plan is doomed before it starts. The only thing in your favor is the fact that Dick has had enough sense to at least put some time and research into his brief, which is more than I can say for the rest of you."

"In other words you think we're all wrong?" asked Boland.

"I didn't say that—I said you were going at it the wrong way. First, I couldn't care less what any of you think of me, especially you, Harry. I've honestly tried to do the best for the work and if I've upset anyone I'm sorry. I won't change my approach for anyone—you can take it or leave it. I know that neither I nor my family are the most popular in the church, but that's the least of my worries."

Hart looked up, "I don't think there is any need to go on further, Alt, we know how you feel. I suggest that we just forget the whole matter and let it die once and for all. What do you say?"

"I think you are out of your mind. One little disagreement and you're ready to throw in the sponge. You are weaker than I thought," said Brent as he moved to get up.

"Wait, Alt, you mean you think it's a good idea?" asked Boland.

"I never said it wasn't, did I?"

"No."

"All right then, let's get down to business."

Chapter 3

HARRISON PHINNAMORE did not consider himself to be a moody individual, in fact, he had always thought he was even-tempered with a placid disposition. To those who knew him best he was the perfect example of one who practiced what he preached, a perfect Christian.

Being a creature of habit he disciplined his time, making sure that every day was well spent in the work of the Lord. Monday was his day for rest and relaxation. He felt that even a minister needed some time to himself. In summer he would usually play a round of golf with one or two retired friends, or take a drive in the country with his wife, Beth, usually ending up for dinner at one of the small, quaint, out-of-the way restaurants which dotted the countryside. The next four days were busily spent visiting the sick and shut-ins, attending to the routine business of the church, conducting the Wednesday evening prayer meeting and just being a pastor to his congregation. Saturdays were devoted to the preparation of the Sunday messages. Weather permitting, he would take his Bible and notes out into the garden and under a large spreading maple tree, prepare his sermons. All in all, Harrison Phinnamore had all that a man could ask for—peace, contentment and the knowledge that he was serving his God to the best of his ability.

He really didn't know what had happened; everything was changing. For months he had been fighting the onslaught of deep depression. Instead of being outgoing he was drawing deeper into himself.

Visiting was sheer torture, he only called when he was forced into it and there was no way out. His sermons were rehashed from old ones, and not very good rehashes at that.

It had been the custom at Fairview for the minister and his wife to stand at the front door and shake hands following the morning service. He had even given that up by assigning the chore to the various elders on a rotation basis. As soon as the benediction was pronounced and the postlude sung he left the platform for the sanctuary of his study where he remained until the congregation had left.

His strange behavior became the subject of conversation at many dinner tables. Some thought he was suffering from a nervous or physical breakdown, while some seriously questioned his relationship with God. Regardless of the questions asked or the answers given the situation was not good. Fairview was obviously affected, and more seriously so were certain individuals who had come to look upon Phinnamore as their spiritual guide and example.

One or two of his closest friends tried to draw him out, but all they got for their efforts was an indifferent shrug and a monosyllabic mumble in reply.

His wife Beth had always made it a policy to remain silent on matters concerning the physical or secular life of the church. She steadfastly refused to be drawn into a debate, regardless of the subject. This had earned her the respect and admiration of the congregation, also the dislike of some of the women members who continually kept up the undercurrent, enjoying nothing better than a good old-fashioned gossip party. Since she refused to participate, even when privately agreeing, that segment of the congregation treated her with polite indifference.

This time, however, she had about decided to renounce her self-imposed vow of silence. It was no secret that her husband was going through difficult times and the bits and pieces of information which she picked up from time to time only reinforced her concern.

Following one particularly trying Sunday morning service she quietly slipped her hand into her husband's as they walked to the car at the rear of the parking lot and gave it an affectionate squeeze.

"Remember the place up near Castle Hill where we stopped and had that lovely meal last fall?" she asked.

"Yes, what about it?"

"Why don't we drive up there for the afternoon and have dinner?"

"What about the dinner at home?"

"It'll only take me a moment to put it back in the refrigerator. It wasn't much to get excited about anyway."

"I don't care, it's up to you."

"I just thought it would be a change," her voice was softly resigned.

Phinnamore didn't reply—instead he wheeled out of the parking lot and down the main street toward home. As he pulled into the driveway and stopped the car he just sat looking straight ahead, not saying anything.

"Harrison, are you all right, what's the matter?"

"Nothing, dear, I was just thinking about how we used to get excited about going out for dinner, now it seems immaterial."

"If you would rather stay home I don't mind."

"No, I think it would do us both good. Don't take long—I'll wait here."

The drive in the country worked wonders. By the time they arrived at the picturesque country restaurant with the sparkling stream flowing at the bottom of a well-trimmed lawn he was a completely changed man. The tired lines in his face had begun to soften and a twinkle began returning to his eyes.

"I'm glad you talked me into this. It's just what I needed. Let's take a walk along the bank before we eat. I'd like to get a breath of clean fresh air, especially some that's not contaminated by idle gossip and innuendos."

Instead of just holding hands he put an arm around his wife's waist and gave it a loving squeeze.

"Harrison, for heaven's sake, what will people think?"

"You don't seem to care **too much**."

"Why?"

"You haven't made me take it away."

They walked for about half an hour, occasionally stopping to look at some flowers or listen to a bird singing.

"We had better start back, I'm getting hungry."

"You're always hungry, but I suppose that's the sign of a growing boy," his wife replied in mock anger.

The restaurant was practically filled but they were fortunate in getting a table for two overlooking the garden and stream.

As soon as the waitress had laid out the dinner and left, Phinnamore picked up his fork and began to eat the salad. His wife looked at him not knowing just what to say.

"Harrison?"

"Yes," he looked up, his mouth full of food.

"Haven't you forgotten something?"

"What?"

"Grace."

"Oh, I thought I'd take a rain check on it and enjoy myself," he lowered his head and began eating.

Rather than upset him or spoil the meal his wife said no more, just quietly bowed her head.

They chatted amicably for the balance of the meal and were just about to begin dessert when Phinnamore looked across the room, his face hardening into a furrowed scowl.

"Do you see who just came in?" he growled half under his breath.

"Where?"

"Over there by the door, don't look up, maybe they won't see us."

"It's too late, dear, here they come." His wife hardly got the words out when a hand was thrust in front of her face toward her husband.

"Pastor, this is a coincidence."

"Hello, Charlie," the greeting was less than enthusiastic.

"Hello, Mrs. Phinnamore."

"Hello, Mr. Scales. How are you, Mildred?"

"Fine, Beth, just fine," she replied.

"Do you mind if we join you?"

15

"We're just finishing, you can have our table," said Phinnamore looking around the room.

"No, we'll all get a table together. You can have your dessert with us."

"It's all right, we must be on our way, it's getting. . . ."

"Won't take no for an answer, will we, Mildred?" He didn't give his wife time to answer, instead beckoned for a waitress.

"Would you please get us a table for four and bring our friends' dessert and coffee to it—they're joining us for dinner."

"Yes sir, I'll clear one off and it'll be ready in a moment."

Phinnamore felt his foot being tapped under the table and looked across at his wife who was near tears. Sensing that she felt more sorry for him than for herself he reached across the table and gave her hand a gentle squeeze.

The waitress placed their dessert and coffee cups on a tray and said, "Will you come this way please?"

As they walked across the room to the rear of the restaurant Phinnamore felt an arm on his shoulder as Scales whispered out of the corner of his mouth, "I want to have a talk with you."

Chapter 4

Dick Hart cleared his throat and after running an index finger around his collar said, "If there's no further business I hereby declare this meeting adjourned."

"Mr. Chairman," the voice came from the back of the room, "I would like to place a motion before the membership."

"The chair recognizes Alton Brent."

All heads turned to watch Brent weave his way through the maze of chairs and stand at the side of the platform.

"Mr. Chairman, fellow members of Fairview. . . ."

His following words were drowned out by a deep-throated voice, "We can't hear you, Alt, speak into the microphone."

Hart motioned with his hand and Brent mounted the small platform, laid some papers on the lectern and said, "Is that better?"

"All right now, Alt," came the reply.

Brent looked around the room for a moment before he spoke. It was better than two-thirds filled, *A remarkable turnout for a business meeting,* he thought. The only answer seemed to be that someone had been doing a good job of contacting the membership. Some of the faces looking up at him had been conspicuous by their absence at regular services for many months. It could only mean one of two things: they either had renewed their interest in Fairview or they were primed to come out with the promise of an exciting evening. He ruled out the former and thought, *If it's excitement they want they couldn't have picked a better meeting.*

"Mr. Chairman, pastor, members of Fairview," Brent began,

picking his words deliberately and slowly. "What I'm about to propose probably won't meet with the approval of everyone here so before we begin I would ask that we all bow our heads and ask God's blessing on what's to follow."

There was a shuffling of feet and one or two nervous coughs. Brent waited for everything to quiet down, then began, "Our dear Heavenly Father, we come to Thee tonight to ask Thy blessing and guidance on the balance of this meeting. Whatever is said or done we pray that it will be to Thy honor and glory, Amen."

"Amen," repeated one or two.

"As an introduction to what I'm about to present I'd like to review, briefly, the history of Fairview Church. I know that there is hardly one in this room who doesn't know what has been accomplished in the past, but if you'll give me your indulgence I'm sure you'll see the point I'm trying to make. Illustrated charts have been prepared which I'll now ask Steve Gordon to bring in and place on the easel."

Gordon went out of the room and returned with a number of full-sized sheets attached to a piece of plywood. As he was placing it on the easel and moving it into position so everyone could see, a middle-aged man halfway back stood up.

"Mr. Chairman."

"The Chair recognizes Harold Smith," responded Hart.

"I realize that another speaker has the floor, but I would like to point out one thing, a very important thing if I may."

Hart looked over at Brent who was standing by the easel talking to Gordon in hushed tones.

"Do you have any objection if Mr. Smith continues?"

"None whatsoever if it will help clarify the situation."

"All right, Mr. Smith, you may continue. I'll instruct the church clerk to record that your interjection was with the full approval of the recognized speaker."

"Thank you," began Smith. "I don't intend to take up very much time, but I think that before anything as serious as this appears to be is continued we should establish that members and members only be allowed to remain in the meeting."

"Just what are you trying to say?" asked Hart.

"Well, it seems to me that according to our constitution only voting members should be allowed to remain."

"This point has never been challenged as long as I've been on the board," said Hart.

"It's about time it was, Mr. Chairman. I move that the roll be called and those who are not formal members of this church be asked to leave."

"Why must they leave? As long as they don't vote on anything, what harm can be done?"

"You don't seem to understand, Mr. Chairman." His face began to flush. "They have to leave, Charlie said. . . ."

Scales seared Smith with a withering glare.

A deathly silence came over the room. Hart finally broke it by shuffling some papers in front of him and said, "Harold Smith has moved that we call the roll and respectfully ask those whose names are not called to absent themselves from the remainder of the meeting. Will someone second the motion?"

He looked around the room. All heads were lowered and he could see from the flushed face of Harold Smith that here was a man who had put his foot in it and would be hearing about his indiscretion later.

"Yes, thank you, Mrs. Mildred Scales has seconded the motion, all in favor please signify in the usual manner, contrary, carried."

He instructed the clerk to call the membership roll, after which there was a movement of bodies as the ranks were thinned by those who left the meeting.

"Now then, would Mr. Brent please continue with his statement?"

"Thank you, Mr. Chairman," replied Brent as he moved over to the easel and flipped the cover page revealing a chart with a number of brightly colored bar graphs.

For the next half hour he traced the rise and fall of Fairview's accomplishments and influence. When he had finished with the charts he returned behind the lectern.

"I think that each of you here will agree that unless something is done and done quickly our church will pass out of existence. I, personally, do not want this to happen neither do the members of the church board. We have given this deep consideration and have agreed on the motion which I'm about to put forward to this assembly."

He held up a paper and began to read. "We, the undersigned members of the Church Council of Fairview Community Church, do hereby make the following motion. Whereas the spiritual condition of the church has deteriorated over the past period of time to a point of grave concern, we move that the membership be instructed to elect a body of men whose duty it shall be to investigate and sound out various qualified ministers and bring recommendations to the membership regarding the issuing of a call."

The meeting erupted into an uproar.

"You see, Charlie was right," bellowed Harold Smith, "they are trying to get rid of Pastor Phinnamore."

Hart rapped the table with his pencil, it had no effect so he rose to his feet and pounded it with his fist.

"Order, order, this meeting will be adjourned immediately if you do not respect the rules of procedure by addressing the chair when you wish to speak. When this motion is completed and a seconder obtained it will be thrown open for comments. You'll all be given an opportunity to be heard. Please continue, Mr. Brent."

"Thank you. The balance of the motion reads as follows. It is not the intention of this committee to cast any reflection on the ability or leadership of the current pastor Reverend Harrison Phinnamore. Rather, it goes on record as commending him for his long and faithful ministry to this pastorate. It is also not the intention of this motion to seek his dismissal, rather recommend that the committee formed seek for a man who would identify with the youth and young people of the church and work in close harmony with Reverend Harrison as an associate minister. On behalf of the Church Committee I move that this motion be accepted."

Brent picked up the papers in front of him and walked off the platform, taking a seat in the second row beside Steve Gordon.

Hart took his position behind the lectern and asked, "Is there a second for this motion?"

No one made a move, each one looking around to see who would put up their hand.

"There must be a second to the motion otherwise it cannot stand for a vote," said Hart.

At the rear of the room someone stood to his feet as all heads turned.

"I'll second that motion, Mr. Chairman."

"Thank you, the motion is moved by Alton Brent and seconded by Robert Harris. Will the clerk please read the motion once again? Then it will be thrown open for discussion."

Following the reading, one after another got to their feet and either supported or criticized the motion including the men behind it. For a while it appeared that things were getting out of hand as personalities entered into the debate.

"Mr. Chairman, I take strong exception to the obvious lobbying which has gone on before this meeting," said George King, the Sunday school superintendent. "It is quite plain that certain factions in this membership have been busy and tried their level best to scuttle this motion before it ever got placed before the meeting."

Before Hart could comment Charlie Scales was on his feet.

"I believe Mr. King is referring to my hand in this matter."

"Are you requesting permission to speak before this meeting? If so please make your intentions known in the proper manner," admonished the chairman.

Scales drew a deep breath and laboriously said, "Mr. Chairman, may I please have the floor?"

"Is Mr. King finished?"

"Yes."

"You have the floor."

"Thank you. As I said, I believe Mr. King is referring to me."

"If the shoe fits, wear it," came a voice.

"Order, I'll not permit this meeting to turn into an open debate."

"Thank you once again, Mr. Chairman. As I said twice before I believe Mr. King was referring to me. To set his mind at ease I'll explain my position. I'm an elected member of the Church Council

21

and as such was invited to a meeting at our Chairman's home a little while back. While there I heard a presentation of practically what was given tonight. Since I did not agree with it I left the meeting. I'm as concerned as anyone else about what's happening to our church, but the personal and character assassination of a servant of God is not my idea of a remedy."

Harry Boland leaped to his feet, "I object to your turn of words—I object strongly."

"Sit down Mr. Boland, Mr. Scales has the floor."

"He'll have the whole building, right on the head if he keeps that up," came the reply.

"I must insist that you refrain from that type of comment or I'll ask the council members to remove you from the meeting."

"I'd like to see them try."

"Harry, please keep quiet, you're no better than they are," breathed his wife.

"I'll keep quiet . . . for the moment," snarled Boland.

"Continue," said Hart nodding to Scales.

"I regret that things have gotten to the point where supposedly Christian men and women have resorted to arena type actions, especially in the House of God. I hope that just because there are differences we will be able to snatch some sanity out of this mess and be better Christians for it. I left the meeting at Mr. Hart's because I respect the pastor and will have no part of a public censure. The charts and figures presented earlier paint a pretty bleak picture of just what we are and where we're heading. I think the idea of someone younger to share the work and relieve the pastor of many of his burdens is a good one. This must have been added after I left the meeting. I'll support it if it's passed tonight. I do suggest, however, that instead of associate pastor he be called assistant pastor and his terms of reference be clearly defined. I also suggest that he be directly responsible to the pastor and not the church board."

"Are you proposing an amendment to the original motion?" asked the chairman.

"Yes."

"Very well, will the clerk record the amendment and we'll vote on it?"

After the clerk had read the motion and the amendment a vote was taken and passed without too much opposition.

One or two more made some comments about the original motion, but they were of little consequence. There was a momentary lull in the meeting and someone called for the question.

"The question has been called for. If there are no objections we'll now vote."

"Mr. Chairman," the speaker was Arthur Bright, a senior member of the congregation.

"Yes, Mr. Bright."

"I've been listening to all the wrangling tonight and it makes me very unhappy to see this in our church. I think that everyone will agree we want the matter settled. So that we can vote on this matter with complete freedom I move that it be a secret vote by ballot."

This motion was seconded and passed without comment. Once the officials had been appointed and ballots distributed the vote was taken.

While the members waited for the results they passed the time singing hymns.

Dick Hart stood to his feet and moved behind the lectern. "The results of the vote are 112 in favor, 48 against. I hereby declare that the motion is carried."

After a debate on the terminology a selection committee was elected. The name pulpit committee was rejected in deference to Phinnamore, who remained stoic and silent through the evening. The five men elected represented a clear division between the two factions, three wholeheartedly supported the Church Committee and the two did not.

"I believe that the evening's business is completed and if there are no objections I move that this meeting be adjourned following a closing prayer by Mr. Steve Gordon," said Hart.

"I'll second that motion," said a weary voice.

"Thank you, Mrs. Wright: all in favor. Contrary? Carried. Mr.

Gordon, will you close in prayer?"

Gordon stood to his feet and began, "Our dear Heavenly Father, we thank Thee that we can gather together as Thy children and work together for Thy glory. We thank Thee for Thy leading and are conscious of Thy hand overshadowing our every word and action tonight. Dismiss us with Thy blessing, in Thy name we ask it. Amen."

Someone snorted!

Chapter 5

THE SIMILARITY BETWEEN twenty-eight-year-old Jimmy Ferguson and Harrison Phinnamore at the same age was striking. Both wore the enthusiasm of youth with bravado.

Jimmy Ferguson was the modern, well-educated minister, one who identified with young people and earned the respect and acceptance of more mature adults.

Ever since he graduated from seminary his progress had been well-planned and steady. First there was a three-month supply period while he filled in for an ailing minister. Next came six months as youth director in one of the larger churches in the city which resulted in a call to be the minister of a small but thriving church in an equally small but thriving town.

In addition to providing valuable training in youth work the six months as youth leader also resulted in his meeting Betty, falling in love and getting married the following summer after he accepted the call.

The similarity between Ferguson and Phinnamore did not stop with their youthful exuberance it was also paralleled in their burning zeal for the things of God. Both completely trusted their Lord for guidance in all matters. The success they enjoyed was ample evidence that they were both God's chosen servants.

The sanctuary was practically filled and as he rose to preach Ferguson could not help but feel a surge of satisfaction. When he had preached his first sermon, it was to less than thirty people. Now, just after a few years it was to more than eight times that number. He acknowledged that without Divine guidance it would probably never have happened. But he was only human, and he also knew that it was the result of honest hard work.

At the rear of the church he noticed two men. They were, as far as he knew, strangers and had never been in the church before.

One was a slight, sandy-haired man in his late twenties or early thirties, the other, heavy-set, older, and with apparent hay fever or allergy problems. He was either wiping his nose or sniffing a small inhaler which was cupped in his hand.

The thing that drew Ferguson's attention to them in the first place was the younger one's reluctance to remove his topcoat. From time to time during the service Ferguson watched as he appeared to be fiddling with something inside it. He was relieved that they sat at the rear of the auditorium and not where they would cause a distraction.

His sermon was entitled "How to Know the Will of God." By way of introduction he said that there probably wasn't a minister who ever lived that had not preached this sermon. He was sure, however, that each one brought something new on the subject and prayed that he would do likewise.

His material was well-prepared and crisply given. The illustrations he sprinkled through the sermon were masterfully chosen and reached all levels of his congregation.

He had always believed that the best sermons were not necessarily the longest ones and made sure that he kept his remarks to the point, never losing the attention of his listeners. He illustrated this point by repeating an old adage given by a seminary professor, "the mind can only absorb what the seat can endure."

Following the benediction as Ferguson and his wife stood at the door shaking hands the two strangers tried to ease past the cluster of people, but Ferguson deliberately excused himself and stepped in front of them.

"It was good of you to join with us this morning. I trust we shall see you again," he said as he shook both hands.

The slighter man spoke up, "Thank you, we'll look forward to it."

Before he could continue his companion interrupted, "I don't see how that will be possible, Reverend, you see we're just passing through."

"Yes, that's right, we're just passing through," repeated the other.

"Well, if you're ever in our vicinity again please come back. Where did you say you came from?"

"We didn't," said the heavier man and before he could continue a woman in a big flowered hat pushed her way between the two men and the minister and took Ferguson by the hand.

"Pastor," she cooed, "that message was just wonderful. I'm so glad some of the members who needed it were here."

"Thank you, Mrs. Dancy, you're very kind."

Ferguson dropped her hand and watched the two men get into their car. He could see from the license plate that they were from out-of-town.

Later as he was sitting down to dinner his wife said, "who were those two men in the service?"

"I don't know, honey. I tried to find out at the front door but Mrs. Dancy interrupted with some of her usual babbling and they left without telling me."

"Did you come right out and ask them?"

"Sure, I thanked them for coming and asked them where they were from."

"Why didn't they tell you?"

"Probably because they didn't want me to know. I think they considered Mrs. Dancy an answer to prayer, because they both looked relieved when she stepped between us."

"If she was, it's the first time in history."

"What's the first time in history?"

"Mrs. Dancy being an answer to prayer."

"Oh."

Harry Boland turned to Gordon, "Where shall I stop for dinner?"

"I don't care, how about the restaurant we passed on the way up here? I don't think it's too far."

"Fine," he replied.

"Sorry about the slip at the door."

"It doesn't matter, Steve. That woman in the floppy hat saved us from an embarrassing situation."

"I just about died when I put my foot in it. Do you think he suspected anything?"

"Probably, but it's too late to do anything about it. Did you get everything?"

"As far as I know. We can listen to the tape as soon as we get home."

"Betty, will you get the mail? I just heard it drop in the box."

"Who was your servant last year? I wish someone would come up with another line: that one's getting worn out, but nevertheless I'll ask it again, who was your servant last year, Pastor Ferguson?" Betty dropped the mail over his shoulder, spewing it across the kitchen table nearly knocking over his cup of coffee.

"If I had a servant last year it certainly must have been a better one than you, my love," he replied as he fished an envelope from under the toaster.

One envelope caught his eye as he leafed through the mail. On it was a line sketch of a Gothic style church with the name Fairview in Old English type underneath.

"Who do we know at Fairview?" he mused, turning the envelope over in his hand.

"Why don't you open it up and find out?"

Ignoring the comment, he ripped it open and began reading.

"What does it say?"

"Just a moment, I'll let you see it."

As his wife fidgeted in her chair he continued to laboriously read the contents, much to her annoyance.

"Aw, come on, Jimmy, what does it say?" she pleaded.

"Nothing much except they want me to preach at both services three weeks from Sunday if I can arrange it."

"Who wrote the letter?"

"A Richard Hart, chairman of the Church Council. Here, read it for yourself," he said sliding the letter across the table.

28

Ferguson watched his wife reading, then suddenly said, "I wonder?"

"What do you wonder?"

"Remember about five or six Sundays ago when those two fellows were at the morning service and we never did find out who they were or where they came from."

"Yes, what's Fairview got to do with them?"

"The thought just came to me that perhaps they were members of a pulpit committee or something."

"Why wouldn't they tell you who they were, if that's what it was?"

"Don't you know anything about church government? If a church wants to get a new minister they usually send someone on a pulpit committee to observe the prospect. They see what he's like in his own church, then report back to the membership with recommendations. That would explain why the short fellow wouldn't take off his topcoat. He probably had a transistor tape recorder and was taping my message."

"Couldn't he have told you after the service? Why be so mysterious?"

"There was no use saying anything. What if the rest of the committee didn't agree with their recommendations, then what?"

"You don't know for sure. I wonder what's happened to their own minister?"

"I wonder? Remember Paul Cook who was at seminary with me?"

"Yes."

"The last I heard, he had a church not too far from Fairview. I think I'll give him a call and see if he knows anything."

"Would you be interested if they were serious?"

"I'd have to think about it carefully. I've never for a moment thought I'd be here the rest of my life and the challenge of a new charge interests me greatly."

"Well, don't jump to conclusions, perhaps they are stuck for a speaker and heard that you were inexperienced and cheap," mocked Betty.

"I may be inexperienced, but I'm not cheap. I couldn't be and

29

support the likes of you," he replied, flicking a tea towel at her legs.

"All right, Mr. Big and Experienced, the dishes won't wash and dry themselves, so until you can get the manse committee to install an automatic dishwasher you're it."

As he moved toward the sink he slipped his arm around his wife's waist giving her a kiss on the cheek.

"Would you go if they wanted me to?"

"What do you think?" she replied as she put both arms around his neck and kissed him tenderly.

Chapter 6

"MAY I HAVE your attention, please? This meeting will now come to order." Dick Hart tapped the lectern with his pencil.

"Thank you. As you were informed in the members' letter this special meeting has been called so that we can hear the report of the selection committee and their recommendations. I'll call upon the chairman to bring his report at this time."

Gerald Coleman stood up at his seat. He was an intense, slow talking man with large bushy eyebrows. Many of the congregation considered him to be the elder statesman of Fairview and sought his advice on many matters. He not only reveled in this attention, he sought it and was visibly hurt if anything of importance was conducted without his knowledge or approval. There were those who resented this attention and publicly accused some members of voting him onto committees out of habit instead of equating his ability with the demands of the job. When it came to voting for Coleman the leading of the Lord didn't seem to matter. Despite the split opinion he was a man of influence and played the part to the hilt.

"Mr. Chairman, fellow members," he intoned, "I deem it an honor, an honor, I say, to have been elected chairman of the selection committee. I wish to thank all my committee members for their outstanding cooperation and untiring work."

A voice whispered, "Get on with the report, we don't want a sermon."

"Stop that," hushed another.

Coleman cleared his voice and looked around. "Since I seem to be taking up someone's valuable time I'll be brief. Unfortunately I was not able to accompany the investigation team on their assignments so I'll call upon Steve Gordon to bring the report on behalf of that group."

Gordon made his way to the front of the room and stood behind the lectern.

"Mr. Chairman, fellow members, as you know our committee was instructed to investigate a number of candidates for the position of assistant minister. We laid down explicit conditions and requirements, then weighed each candidate's qualifications against them. I might say that one by one we quickly eliminated the various names which were brought forward. For one reason or another they didn't measure up to what we felt the Lord would have for our church. After weeks of investigation and prayer we narrowed a list of twenty-seven names down to three. Once we agreed on these men it was decided that each one should be visited and observed, unannounced in his own church. Two were ruled out because of personality problems. The third, in our unanimous opinion, is the man for Fairview. His name is Reverend James Ferguson. During the visit that Harry Boland and I made to his church we were able to tape the morning service. I would like to play part of his sermon for you all to hear before I outline his background and qualifications. I'll ask Harry to bring the tape recorder to the front at this time."

For the next twenty to twenty-five minutes everyone in the room strained to hear what had been recorded. One by one the expressions on their faces changed from indifference to acceptance, and by the time Boland clicked the machine off it was apparent that the majority had been won over.

Gordon followed the tape with an outline of Ferguson's background, both personal and spiritual. He then presented a motion that Ferguson be called to fill the position of assistant minister. The motion was quickly seconded and then thrown open for discussion.

Charlie Scales was the first to speak, "Mr. Chairman, we have just witnessed a masterful selling job and I applaud the selection committee, and particularly Mr. Gordon. One point, however, disturbs me very much and that is the fact that no one has had the common decency to ask the one man who will be most affected his opinion. I'm referring to Reverend Phinnamore, our pastor."

Everyone turned to look at the Phinnamores who were seated as inconspicuously as possible at the side of the room. Mrs. Phinnamore leaned over and whispered in her husband's ear. He did not stir and it looked as though he was miles away in thought. She whispered again and he placed both hands on the chair in front and stood to his feet.

"Mr. Chairman," his voice was unsteady and unsure. "I had no intention of speaking about this matter tonight, but my wife thinks that it is time I did speak. Not only for my own personal interest, but for the good of Fairview which I love so dearly. I've carried on all these months while unrest and discord has raged about because I believe the Lord would have me do so. I'm not oblivious to the fact that much of the problem is my fault and mine alone. Each day that passes convinces me more and more how inadequate I am. I would point out, however, that some of you are not blameless either. The Lord has given us this corner of His vineyard to work in and I'm sorry to say that for the past while there has been more gossip, unrest and trouble-making than work. Regardless of who's to blame we must all shoulder the responsibility This new man, James Ferguson, sounds like he could be the man God is sending to bring a fresh breath of air into our midst. I for one will welcome his arrival and pray that together we two, with God's help, may bring Fairview back to the place of spiritual blessing it once enjoyed." Instead of sitting down he took his wife's hand and raising her up, walked out of the room.

No one spoke!

Betty Ferguson was like a young bride again. It wasn't too many months since she had been, but the thrill of moving into their first real home excited her until she nearly burst.

Ever since she and Jimmy were married they had either lived in a small apartment or rented flat. Now they were going to have a house all to themselves. One of the things that made them decide to accept the call to Fairview was the offer of a house, plus a liberal car allowance. There were other considerations such as the

33

challenge and of course the leading of the Lord, but who could blame them? It was a step forward in Ferguson's career.

Once they had decided to make the move they were caught up in a tumult of activity. The parting at their old church was tinged with sadness. They were genuinely sorry to leave, but the congregation realizing that they could not hope to hang on to someone of Ferguson's potential accepted his decision without rancor.

Shortly after receiving the official call from Fairview, Ferguson contacted his former classmate and asked him to look into the situation and let him know what he found out. The report was less than glowing as he told of the open unrest in the church and the hostility toward the minister from certain factions.

Armed with this information, Ferguson decided to contact Phinnamore and have a talk with him, but before he could, Phinnamore called him and arranged a meeting.

Betty rushed around all morning sweeping and resweeping the tiny apartment until finally, in sheer desperation her husband said, "Sit down Betty, you'll wear the floor out."

"It's all very well for you to sit there and meditate, but I'm the one whose reputation is at stake."

"How do you figure that?"

"Men don't care what the place looks like but women do. If Mrs. Phinnamore is like most women she'll decide whether or not she likes me by how clean I keep my house."

"Nonsense."

"Nonsense, nothing. I know how women think. After all, I'm one myself, or have you been too busy to notice?"

Before he could reply there was a knock at the apartment door.

"They're here. Do I look all right?"

"You look just fine, now settle down, they're not going to bite you."

"Want to bet?"

Ferguson opened the door with his wife at his side.

"Hello, we're so glad you could come. This is my wife, Betty."

Phinnamore shook Ferguson's hand warmly. "We're pleased you asked us. I'd like you to meet Mrs. Phinnamore."

After the introductions were completed, the two women left the men and went into the kitchen while Betty prepared dinner.

Ferguson and Phinnamore took an immediate liking to each other as did their wives and were quickly on a first name basis. It was not very long until Phinnamore told his younger colleague the events which had led up to his being called to Fairview and his relief at finally having someone who would not only share the work, but the burdens associated with it.

As is the case with all good pastors Phinnamore attempted to remain objective about everything and keep personalities out of the discussion, but as one name after another cropped up it was plain that some individuals suddenly became subjective.

"Do you realize that you two have never stopped talking since you walked through the door?" asked Betty as she announced that dinner was ready.

"My dear," replied Mrs. Phinnamore, "this is the first time in ages that I've seen Harrison say more than two words to anyone. It's a refreshing change."

Phinnamore put his arm around his wife. "What about all the nights I kept you awake talking?" he chided.

"They don't count. Anyway, I wish you wouldn't tell me just part of the story. Ever have your husband start a good tale then say that he could tell you more but he can't?"

"I sure have," laughed Betty. "I've reached the place where I tell Jimmy to forget it if he can't finish it."

"Good girl, a woman after my own heart," laughed Mrs. Phinnamore.

The rest of the day was spent in getting to know each other better. By the time the Phinnamores left it was evident that both couples were looking forward to a pleasant relationship in the future.

Betty was ecstatic. "Aren't they just wonderful?" she said.

"Yes, I like them both, but he's a man that's been completely shattered. I feel sorry for him," replied her husband.

"Why, just because there's been some trouble in the church?"

"No, it's more than that. I honestly think we're walking into something. I can't put my finger on it, but I know it's there."

35

"You're just imagining it."

"Well, have your own way, it should prove interesting."

It was just the week before Ferguson preached his farewell sermon. The church held a going-away dinner and presented them with a large family Bible in remembrance. The warmth of their wishes touched them both, and as is often the case in a situation such as this they began to have second doubts about leaving a secure environment for something as uncertain as Fairview appeared to be.

Betty was all alone in the apartment surrounded by packing cases when the telephone rang.

"Mrs. Ferguson?" the voice was deep and husky.

"Yes."

"Is your husband at home?"

"No, he isn't, I expect him shortly."

"Will you give him a message for me, please?"

"Certainly."

"Tell him to be careful and watch who he makes friends with at Fairview."

"Who is this? What do you want?"

"Never mind, it's in your husband's interest to go slowly and trust no one. Remember, he was warned."

Betty could hear someone breathing at the other end of the line.

"Who are you? Why don't you tell me?"

Instead of an answer the line went dead with an ominous click. Betty just sat transfixed, staring at the phone with the receiver in her hand. The turning of a key in the door brought her back to reality.

As her husband came into the living room she ran toward him, throwing her arms around his neck.

"Oh Jimmy, it was awful, that horrible man on the telephone. Tell them we won't go, tell them we changed our minds. Oh Jimmy, it was awful!" She buried her head in his shoulder and started to sob.

It took Ferguson some time to calm his wife and get a coherent recount of exactly what had happened.

36

"Don't worry about it—probably some practical joker," he tried to reassure her but not very convincingly.

Later that night after they had gone to bed they were awakened by the telephone. Ferguson reached for his dressing gown and stumbled into the living room, stubbing his toe on a packing case.

"Hello."

There was no answer, just the heavy breathing of someone at the other end.

"Hello, who is this?"

Still no answer.

"Listen," Ferguson was getting angry and his voice betrayed his emotions, "whoever you are, I'm a bit sick of this nonsense. If you have something to say, say it, if not hang up."

The voice was deep and precise, "Did your wife give you a message?"

"So it's you, is it? The next time you phone and upset my wife I'll call the police. What kind of nut are you?"

"No nut I assure you, Reverend Ferguson, just a simple person concerned about his church. Remember my warning. Be sure to pick your friends at Fairview. Not everyone wants you."

"What do you. . . ?" the line went dead.

"Who was it, Jimmy?"

"Go back to sleep, it was a wrong number."

Chapter 7

It DIDN'T TAKE Ferguson long to fit in. Within a few weeks he was making a noticeable contribution to the work at Fairview. His enthusiasm and willingness to accept responsibility quickly endeared him to the congregation and with one or two exceptions he was accepted without qualification.

Phinnamore also had taken on a new outlook. His attitude had drastically changed and he was once again becoming the Phinnamore of old, the man so many looked up to and respected.

So that there would be no conflict or misunderstanding the two men agreed to conduct their relationship in terms of business. Each one wrote out a job description wherein they listed what they thought their area of responsibility was, then met and after a lengthy discussion agreed to each one's terms of reference.

One aspect of the work which had suffered to the point of almost disappearing, especially during Phinnamore's low period, was the youth activities. There was absolutely nothing organized to bridge the gap between the twelve-year-olds and the young people's group which started at sixteen.

Keith Ram, a volatile redhead, was the leader of the young people's organization. He had the respect of the teenage crowd and by various means of manipulation from cajolery to downright social blackmail had managed to hold the group together, and in fact had been the means of it growing and prospering in spite of the difficulties.

The in-between group was another matter. Phinnamore, deeply concerned, realized his limitations at reaching this age and decided that Ferguson's first challenge in the work would be heading up a new organization. He tentatively called it "Intermediates."

He made a survey of the membership and when he had all his facts and plan of operation clearly framed out he asked Ferguson to meet with him in his office.

Ferguson was delighted with the suggestion and wanted to get started right away. This was fine with Phinnamore, but with one exception. He had always believed in covering himself at all times if possible and suggested that the leadership of the new organization should be a joint one shared by Ferguson, his wife and another couple. In this manner, he felt, there would always be a leader available. The women could sub-head the girls, and the men the boys, with both couples being jointly responsible for the overall planning. Ferguson was delighted. Betty had expressed a desire to become active in the work and this would be her opportunity.

The other couple Phinnamore suggested was Steve and Muriel Gordon. He had already spoken to the Gordons and they were as eager to get started as the Fergusons.

Once the pastor and his assistant agreed on the overall format for the organization Phinnamore stepped out of the picture and left it up to the two couples to work out the details.

Gordon pushed the door open with his foot. "Come on in," he said. "I'll just put these parcels in the kitchen."

Ferguson and his wife followed Muriel Gordon into the living room while her husband, arms filled with grocery bags, disappeared into the kitchen.

"Make yourself comfortable, I'll only be a moment. If I don't watch Steve he'll dump everything on the table and it'll still be there in the morning."

"That's all right, can I help?" asked Betty.

"No thanks," replied Muriel over her shoulder as she left the room.

Ferguson was seated on the chesterfield and looked over at his wife.

"What are they doing out there?" she whispered.

"Why don't you go out and see if you're so curious?"

"You're no help. I just wonder. . . ."

She stopped talking in the middle of a word as both the Gordons came into the room.

"Hope you didn't mind us picking up a few groceries on the way back from the church?" asked Gordon.

"No, not at all," replied Ferguson.

"Muriel and I thought it was high time we got together on a social basis; after all we've been involved with Intermediates for quite a while now."

"Good idea. Betty and I feel guilty at not having you two over, but with moving and all we've been pretty busy."

Both girls looked at each other and laughed self-consciously.

That was to be the beginning of many evenings which slowly nurtured a binding friendship between the two couples. They could hardly have been more different. The Fergusons were outgoing and friendly, the Gordons distant and sometimes aloof, particularly Steve. Muriel left all decisions up to her husband and seldom ventured an opinion, much to the annoyance of Betty, who was outspoken and plainly had a mind of her own.

Phinnamore was just getting into his car at the rear of the church parking lot when Ferguson drove up to the back door and honked the horn.

"I came as soon as I could," he called out of the side window. "What's the matter?"

Phinnamore jumped out of his car and rushed up the back steps of the church. "Come into the office," he shouted over his shoulder.

Ferguson followed him through the deserted Sunday school auditorium in silence, their footsteps echoing in the emptiness. As they reached the pastor's office he noticed that the door was partly open and wondered about it because Phinnamore was a stickler about keeping everything locked up.

"There are valuable church papers in the files and, more important, letters and information about various members which is privileged communication and for no one's eyes but mine," he once said when issuing instructions about the necessity of never leaving the office unlocked.

As they reached the office Ferguson said, "The door's open."

Phinnamore didn't reply, rather pushed it open as wide as it could go and switched on the light.

"Good night!" Ferguson gasped. "What happened?"

"You tell me?"

The office was a shambles, drawers were turned upside down on the floor. The filing cabinet was lying on its side as if someone was looking for something underneath.

Phinnamore slumped down in his arm chair and swiveled around to face his young companion.

"What do you think of this mess?"

"I can't believe it. Who would want to do a thing like this? Surely no one is stupid enough to think there was money here?"

"It wasn't money they were after, at least not in currency."

Ferguson picked up a toppled chair and sat down. "What do you mean, at least not in currency?"

Phinnamore ignored the question and began to straighten up the disarrayed papers on his desk. Ferguson noticed that his hands were shaking.

"I don't think you should touch anything until the police arrive."

Phinnamore exploded, "The police won't be coming."

"Why not? This is a criminal offense, they should be called."

"They're not going to be called. Is that clear?"

Ferguson looked at the man behind the desk. There were tiny beads of sweat standing out on his forehead and his face was flushed.

"Did you hear me, Jim?"

"Yes, I heard you, but I don't like it."

Phinnamore began to shuffle the papers again.

"Here let me do it. Why don't you get the kettle out of the cupboard and make us a cup of coffee? I'll stay with you and we'll clean it up together."

Phinnamore dropped the papers and slowly stood up. "It's times like this that I'm sorry I'm involved in this. I knew it would happen sooner or later."

"Knew what would happen?"

"This, I just knew it. They're never satisfied."

41

Phinnamore stumbled out of the office with the electric kettle and headed down the hall toward the washroom. Ferguson started to pick up the scattered files. He noticed that they were tabbed with names, members' names instead of the expected church titles such as Sunday school, missions and so forth.

Phinnamore burst into the room. "Just leave those, I'll put them away; just leave those files for me."

"I was only trying to help."

"You start on the books and put them back on the shelves. I'll straighten up the file cabinet."

Ferguson handed the older man the files he was holding and reached into a cupboard for two cups and a jar of instant coffee.

"Why don't we stop for a moment and have coffee? It'll do us both good."

Phinnamore plopped into his chair. "Yes, that's a good idea!"

The two men drank their coffee in silence and were just about finished when the solitude was broken by the harsh ring of the telephone. Phinnamore didn't move to answer it, instead he just stared at it.

"Aren't you going to answer it?" asked Ferguson.

"No, you answer it."

A look of relief came over his face when he heard Ferguson say, "Hello. Yes Betty."

"Jimmy, what's going on?" Betty's voice was strained. "Mrs. Phinnamore's just about worried sick."

"Nothing, honey, just going over some program outlines. Don't wait up for me—I'll be a little late."

"Jimmy, are you all right?"

"Yes, certainly."

"Can't you talk?"

"That's right, some program outlines."

"What will I tell Mrs. Phinnamore?"

"Can you?"

"Can I talk? Yes, she's in the bathroom and doesn't know I'm calling."

"Well don't keep it for me. I'll get a bite before I come home."

Jimmy was thankful that Betty caught on to what he was trying to say.

"You don't want me to say anything to her, is that right?"

"Yes, don't worry about something to eat. I'll be all right." Ferguson winked at Phinnamore.

"Jimmy, I have to go, she's coming downstairs."

Betty dropped the telephone in the cradle.

"Was that Harrison on the telephone?"

"No, Mrs. Phinnamore, I thought it would be nice to have some Chinese food sent in and we could have dinner together," she lied.

"What did you order?"

Betty swallowed. "Nothing, I thought you might like to decide so I said I'd call back."

"I'm not fussy, whatever you like."

"Say, I've an idea. Why don't we go out and let them wait on us for a change? I like the idea of being served, saves washing dishes." She attempted an uneasy laugh.

"Well, I suppose so. It sounds like you're stuck with me for the evening. I don't know what got into Harrison. All of a sudden he told me to get ready because he was dropping me off at your house for the evening."

Betty tried to appear uninterested. "Did he say what was wrong?"

"No, he just said he was going to the church and I was to wait here for him, that's all."

"You don't seem to know any more than I do. Shall we go?"

The two women got their coats and were just going out the door when the telephone started ringing.

"You might as well go out to the car, I'll see who it is."

Betty took off her gloves and picked up the receiver, "Hello."

There was no immediate answer, just the hollow echo of an open line.

"Hello, who is this?"

With a chilling fear, the memory of those earlier telephone calls flashed back.

43

"Mrs. Ferguson," the voice was rasping and slightly muffled.

"Yes." Betty tried to keep complete control and not betray her emotions.

"Your husband doesn't listen too well, does he?"

"What—what do you mean?"

"I thought that he was smarter than he is!"

Betty suddenly straightened up. "You listen to me, whoever you are. Unless you are sick I suggest you quit this little charade. I . . . ."

The voice on the other end of the line cut her off. "Really, Mrs. Ferguson, hysterics no less. Let me assure you that I'm not sick and I'm not playing games. Tell your husband that the next time I have to call he'll wish he'd listened to me and stayed out of something that's none of his business." The line snapped dead.

She was jolted back to reality by a voice.

"Betty, what's keeping you? Was that Harrison?"

"Oh, Mrs. Phinnamore, no, it was just a neighbor of mine asking me to join her and some of the girls for coffee tomorrow morning." It wasn't nearly as difficult to lie this time.

"This is the last," said Ferguson as he handed Phinnamore a pile of file folders.

"Just put them on the desk for a moment, I'm nearly through."

"Whatever it was they were looking for must have been important."

"I'm sorry I can't tell you more, but some day perhaps you'll understand why I want to handle this myself and keep everything quiet."

"If there is any way I can help, all you have to do is ask."

Phinnamore looked at Ferguson intently. "Do you really mean that, Jimmy?"

"Yes, of course I do."

"Well there is one thing I'll ask of you then."

"What is it?"

"Your solemn promise not to mention a word of what happened here tonight to anyone, including Betty."

"Including Betty?"

"Yes, particularly Betty. You saw what they can do and for your sake and especially Betty's you are not to open your mouth to anyone. Understand?"

Ferguson swallowed hard. "Who are they?"

"I've told you too much already." Phinnamore's voice was hard and cruel.

"I don't think it's fair to ask me to keep silent when I know so little about what's going on."

Phinnamore's face softened. "It would be far more unfair for me to tell you anything else. I refuse to discuss it with you after we leave this room. Let's just forget it. O.K.?"

"All right, if you feel that strongly about it."

"I do. One thing more."

"Yes."

"If you ever tell anyone you were here with me tonight I'll have to deny it."

"You'll what?"

"Sorry, Jimmy, that's the way it's got to be."

Ferguson took his eyes away from Phinnamore's. He was going to say something about honesty, but thought better of it. Instead he decided to change the subject.

He looked at his watch and said, "It's nearly ten thirty, I didn't realize it was so late."

"Not in a hurry are you?" asked Phinnamore.

"No, I told Betty to forget dinner and expect me when I got home. Did you suspect something was going to happen?"

"You mean like this?"

"Yes. You don't seem terribly surprised."

"As I told you before you'll understand everything when I can tell you more."

"Just like the old hymn, eh?"

"What hymn?"

"We'll Understand It Better By and By."

Phinnamore laughed quietly. "If it was only that simple."

Ferguson reached for his jacket which he had hung over a chair. "I told Betty not to worry about something to eat. How about dinner?"

45

Phinnamore stood up. "Good idea. Let's get the biggest steak in town on me."

"You're on; it's time we got out of here and forgot this mess."

Phinnamore put his arm around the shoulder of his companion. "That's what I like, an ambitious man with a short memory."

Phinnamore flicked off the switch and locking the door followed Ferguson down the hall toward the Sunday school auditorium. Just as they were leaving the hall the muffled ring of the telephone broke the silence.

Ferguson turned around to look at Phinnamore who was rooted to the spot, his face ashen. "Let it ring—probably a wrong number."

"I'd better answer it. Wait for me in the car, I'll only be a moment."

Phinnamore spun on his heel and rushed to the office door which he unlocked and burst through, slamming it behind him. Ferguson was just about to head for the parking lot when his curiosity got the better of him and he stealthily eased his way down the hall until he was outside the door. From the office he could hear a muffled voice which became clearer as he pressed his ear to the panel.

". . . stupid thing to do." Phinnamore's voice went silent for a moment then began. "Of course I haven't told anyone and I don't intend to. You pull one more stunt like this and I'm through."

Ferguson pressed his ear closer. There wasn't a sound and he was beginning to wonder what was going on. Then Phinnamore started again.

"All right, you've made it plain. I couldn't care less who you are. You'd better remember one thing, you need me more than I need you, so lay off."

Ferguson moved away from the door and quickly ran out of the building as quietly as he could. Once he was in the car he had to grip the steering wheel tightly with both hands to stop shaking.

Phinnamore suddenly appeared at the open window beside Ferguson and said, "I don't feel too good. Do you mind if we forget the steaks? I'd like to go home."

"No, I don't feel too good either. Who was on the phone?"

"No one, just a wrong number."

46

Chapter 8

CHARLIE SCALES was dead!

His body lay sprawled on a pile of choir gowns like a giant puppet whose strings had been cut by an invisible hand.

"How long has he been dead, Doc?"

"Can't really say, Inspector, until the autopsy, but my guess would be twelve to fifteen hours."

Inspector Potter screwed up his forehead and looked at his watch. "Let's see. It's nine thirty in the morning so that would put the time of death somewhere between six and ten o'clock last night. Sound right to you?"

The coroner didn't look up from his squatting position beside the body. "It's as good a guess as you'll get out of me at this point."

"Thanks a lot. What did he die of?"

"Heart failure."

The uniformed officer at the door laughed, but quickly stifled it when he saw the scowl on Potter's face.

"Come on, Doc, cut out the comedy. This is going to be bad enough without having to put up with your lame attempts at humor."

The coroner straightened up and lit the cigarette which had been dangling in his mouth for the last five minutes. "All right," he said, squinting through a haze of smoke, "you want to know what he died of? Well, my report will state that death was due to multiple fractures of the parietal and occipital bones plus an exposed cranial cavity. There were also severe scalp lacerations and contusions."

Potter looked disgusted. "So that's what your report will say. Now what is all that loosely translated into everyday language?"

The coroner's eyes twinkled. "For the likes of you it means that our friend here got his brains knocked out by person or persons unknown wielding a blunt instrument."

"Thank you, Doctor Watson," replied Potter.

"Anything further, Inspector?"

"No, nothing I can think of. I'd appreciate, however, receiving a copy of your coroner's report as quickly as possible. Will you be doing the autopsy?"

"As far as I know. In any case I'll be on hand; this one interests me."

"Will you get that report to me as soon as you can, too?"

"Sure. O.K. if I have the body removed?"

Potter looked over at the photographer who was standing by the door talking to the constable. "Got everything you want, Mark?"

"I'm finished in here unless there's something else?"

"No, that's all. O.K. Doc, you can take him away."

The coroner beckoned to the officer at the door. "Would you please tell the morgue attendants they can have him now."

"Yes sir."

Phinnamore took the sobbing woman's arm and led her through the inner door of the morgue. "There now, Mildred, it's all over."

"What will I do? My Charles is gone. What will I do?"

A uniformed officer who accompanied Phinnamore to the Scales' home touched the minister's arm. "Should I call a doctor?"

Phinnamore shook his head. "I've already called her family physician and he will meet us at her home. My wife's on her way there as well. Can we get her out of here now?"

"Yes, by all means. She made the identification and there's nothing more for her to do at this time."

Mrs. Scales had sat down in a chair while the two men talked, her shoulders convulsing as she sobbed silently to herself.

"We can go now, Mildred. The officer will drive us home."

Phinnamore gently helped her out of the chair as the officer stood nearby in case he needed help.

"Who would do such a dreadful thing to Charles? He was a good man. Who would want to hurt him?" She asked the questions more of herself than anyone in particular.

"I can't answer that, Mildred. The police are working as hard as they can to find the guilty party. Beth will stay with you as long as you need her."

As the three people slowly walked out the door one of the morgue attendants looked after them indifferently and said to his partner. "They come, they go, but what a way to go."

Betty Ferguson shook her husband, "Jimmy, wake up, it's the police."

"The what?" he mumbled, rubbing the sleep out of his eyes.

"The police. He said something terrible has happened at the church and they want you."

Ferguson was fully awake and, reaching for his robe which was hanging on a chair, leaped out of bed. In the living room a uniformed officer uncomfortably twirled his hat around a couple of fingers.

As Ferguson entered the room he said, "Reverend Ferguson?"

"Yes, officer."

"Could you please get dressed and come with me?"

"Yes, but what's the matter?"

Betty broke in, "What do you want my husband for? What's he done?"

"Betty, be quiet," shushed her husband.

"We don't want your husband like that, Mrs. Ferguson. There's been an accident at the church and Inspector Potter wants to talk to him."

"What kind of accident, officer?" asked Ferguson.

The constable shuffled his feet. "Well, it's Mr. Scales. He's dead."

Betty bit the back of her hand and gasped, "Charlie Scales, how?"

"We don't know yet, Mrs. Ferguson. That's why the Inspector

wants to see your husband and anyone else who could tell us something."

"I'll be right with you," said Ferguson, taking off his robe as he went out of the room.

"How can my husband help?"

"I don't know. All the Inspector said was that he wants to talk with anyone connected with the church."

"All right, officer, let's go. I'll call you as soon as I can." Ferguson kissed his wife on the cheek and followed the officer out the door and into the cruiser.

Steve Gordon pushed his way through the crowd which had gathered around the rear door of the church and spilled out into the parking lot. It took a few moments of strenuous pushing for him to reach the door, during which time he parried questions about what had happened with a curt, "I don't know."

The door partly opened in answer to his knocking and a uniformed officer said, "I'm sorry, sir, no one can come in unless it's on official business."

"I'm Stephen Gordon. I was asked to come here by an Inspector Potter."

The door opened further. "Yes, Mr. Gordon, will you come right this way, please?" Noticing the pressing crowd the officer opened the door as wide as possible and announced, "You all might as well go home. There's nothing for you to see."

Someone shouted from the rear, "Has there really been a murder in the church?"

"I've told you all I know," answered the officer, exasperation apparent in his voice. He closed the door without saying anything further and turned to face Gordon.

"Where's the inspector?"

"He's using the minister's study for the time being; right this way, sir."

As they reached the hall outside Phinnamore's office Gordon noticed that a row of chairs had been placed along the wall. It took him a moment to adjust to the reduced lighting from the blazing sun. Before he could clearly make out who was seated, the unmistakable voice of Harry Boland broke through, "Looks like a council meeting. The only one missing is Brent. The way they are acting they probably have a warrant out for him."

Gordon plopped down in an empty chair beside Boland. "What happened?" he asked.

"Haven't you heard? Charlie's been murdered," replied Boland.

"Who said it was murder?"

"Well it certainly wasn't suicide. I heard the morgue attendant say that the back of his head was bashed in."

"What are they doing now?"

"Questioning anyone who has an official position in the church. Ferguson is in with Potter now."

"Anyone say who did it?"

"Not that I've heard."

"How come Charlie was at the church last night? There wasn't a meeting."

"Beats me, all I know is what I've told you."

Phinnamore came through the door from the Sunday school auditorium and walked right past the row of people. He stopped before his study door and spoke to the officer in muted tones.

Boland shrugged his shoulders and gave Gordon a quizzical look as both men watched.

The officer took an envelope from Phinnamore, tapped on the office door and went inside. Moments later he reappeared and whispered something in the minister's ear. He looked pensive for a moment then slowly turned and took a seat at the end of the row beside Gordon.

Boland leaned in front of Gordon. "What was that all about?" he said, nodding his head toward the officer.

Phinnamore looked strained, "Nothing in particular. The Inspector's questioning Jimmy and asked me to look up some information after I took Mildred home from the morgue."

"Is your wife with her?" asked Gordon.

"Yes, I've also called the doctor. She's in pretty bad shape."

Everyone looked up as the door opened and Ferguson came out into the hall. He walked by those seated without saying a word and left the church.

"Will you please go in, Mr. Gordon?" asked the officer.

"Good luck, Steve," called Boland.

He didn't answer, instead walked past the policeman and into the office.

"Have a seat, Mr. Gordon." Potter waved his arm and returned his gaze to a pile of papers spread out on the desk.

Gordon sat down and nervously crossed his legs.

Potter looked up. "Well, Mr. Gordon, it's a nasty business, isn't it?"

"Yes, I suppose it is."

"Have you heard very much about what's happened?"

"No, not very."

"What have you heard?"

Gordon cleared his throat, "Charlie Scales was murdered— that's all."

Potter fixed him with an intent stare. "Murdered, who told you that?"

"They were talking."

Potter stood up and walked to the window. "There it is again."

"There's what again?"

"The mystical 'they.' It appears in every case."

"Would you please be more specific? I'm not interested in generalities. I want the name of the person who told you Mr. Scales was murdered."

"He was, wasn't he?"

"That's not the question. The question is who are 'they' that said he was?"

Gordon looked uncomfortable.

"Come now, Mr. Gordon, unless we have complete frankness at all times we'll never get to the bottom of this, will we? Now I'll ask you once again. Who was it that said Mr. Scales was murdered?"

"Harry Boland."

Potter returned to the desk and looked at the paper Phinnamore had supplied him listing all the officers of Fairview and indicating which ones had a key to the church. "Oh yes, Mr. Boland. I haven't seen him yet. Did he say how he knew that our friend was done in?"

Gordon cleared his throat once again. "Yes, he said he heard one of the morgue attendants talking."

"Well now, we'll have to look into that, won't we?"

Gordon didn't answer.

Potter took out his pipe. "Don't mind if I light up, do you?"

"No, I don't mind."

"Thank you. I think so much better when I have my friend here lit up." Potter laboriously reamed out the bowl with a penknife and carefully packed in fresh tobacco.

It seemed to Gordon that it took him ages to finally get the thing going satisfactorily.

Through a haze of blue smoke Potter said, "Where were you last night between six and ten in the evening, Mr. Gordon?"

"At home."

"Anyone with you?"

"Yes, my wife."

"Anyone else?"

"What is this, do you suspect me?"

"No one's talking about suspecting anyone. All I want to know is whether or not anyone else saw you at home last night?"

"No, I was alone with my wife."

"Thank you, Mr. Gordon—that will be all for now."

"For now, Inspector, does that mean you'll want me again?"

"Probably, Mr. Gordon, probably. Will you ask your friend Mr. Boland to come in, please?"

Gordon stopped in front of Boland, "You're next, Harry."

Betty Ferguson was sitting in front of the living room window and jumped to her feet as she saw her husband getting out of a taxi. Before he could get his key out she threw the door open.

"What kept you so long? I've been worried sick."

"Let me sit down for a moment and catch my breath." Ferguson appeared haggard.

Betty followed him into the living room. "Was Mr. Scales murdered? I've been listening to the news on the radio and they said the police suspect foul play."

"It's foul play all right, about as foul as it can get. I don't know too much else except that I'm probably a prime suspect."

53

"Where are Steve and Mr. Phinnamore? I called Muriel and she said that Steve telephoned to say that he would be a while yet. Did you talk to them?"

"No, I saw them but didn't feel like talking."

"Why not?"

"I just didn't, that's why not."

Betty knew better than to push him further. "What did the police ask you?"

"Betty, I've just come through a session of questions. Give me a break, will you?"

"All right, I'll leave you alone if that's what you want." Her voice quivered and she blinked back the tears.

Ferguson knew he had hurt her and getting up took her in his arms, "Come on sit down. I'll tell you all that happened."

"Mr. Boland, have a seat, I'll be with you in a moment."

Potter picked up the telephone and dialed.

"This is Inspector Potter. Is Sergeant Mullen there, please?"

"Doug, Potter. Will you check something for me? I want to find out what time the prowl car came by Fairview Community Church last night between six and eleven. Call the station responsible for this area and get me a complete report. Have the officers in my office for questioning at four this afternoon. Oh yes, Doug, one further thing, check with communications and see if there were any calls from within a ten block area of the church. Yes, as soon as possible. I'll be here until at least one. Call me back."

He dropped the receiver with a thud. "Mr. Boland. Thank you for coming."

"I didn't have much choice, did I?"

"Well, no," replied Potter rubbing his chin, "you really didn't. But thanks anyway."

"What can I do for you?"

"Well first you could help me clear up a nagging irritation that's been bothering me all morning."

"What's that?"

"I understand that you consider this murder. Is that right?"

"Certainly it's murder, what else could you call it?"

"It could be an accident?"

"Come on now, Inspector, the morgue attendant said that Charlie's brains were knocked out. How could that be an accident?"

Potter smiled and tapped his pipe on the rim of the ash tray. "I once investigated an apparent homicide which turned out to be an accident pure and simple. The victim fell backwards and hit his head on the curb causing practically the same injuries as received by Mr. Scales."

"Oh!"

"Yes, oh, Mr. Boland. The result of that investigation cleared the name of an innocent man who was under suspicion unjustly. Get my point?"

Boland flushed. "I'm sorry, I guess I was shooting my mouth off without thinking."

"That's all right, now let's proceed. I don't want to keep you any longer than I have to."

Potter put Boland through practically the same down-keyed questioning he had given the others, and as he finished he said, "Well, you have been a real help, thanks very much."

"Can I go now?"

"Yes, just leave your home and business telephone number with the officer."

Boland got up and started for the door when Potter held up his hand. "Just one thing further, Mr. Boland. When was the last time you were at the church?"

"At the prayer meeting last Wednesday."

"You haven't been here since?"

"Well, not inside. I was by last night but just in the car."

"Have a seat, Mr. Boland."

"I thought you were finished."

"I will be shortly. Now tell me what time was it? Did you notice anything?"

Boland thought for a moment. "I was on my way home from bowling, it was between ten and eleven when I drove past the church. I always look closely at the building at night. Sometimes there is a light left on or window open. If there is I stop. As I was coming around the corner I noticed a car in the parking lot and was just about to stop when I saw it was Jimmy Ferguson's."

"How did you know it was Ferguson's?"

"Simple, I saw him run out of the church and hop into it."

"Run out of the church?"

"Yes, run."

"Did you stop?"

"No, it was late and I figured he was rushing home."

"Didn't you think it strange that he was there at that time?"

"No, he often works late."

"Thank you, Mr. Boland, I'll get in touch if I need anything further."

"If there is anything else all you have to do is give me a call."

"Thank you, Mr. Boland, you've been most helpful." Potter opened the door and escorted Boland out into the hall.

"Officer, come in for a moment."

"Yes sir."

Potter sat down behind the desk and rubbed his hands together, "Go pick up Reverend James Ferguson and bring him to my office. I'll meet you there in about an hour."

"Arrest him?"

"I didn't say anything about arresting him . . . yet!"

Chapter 9

PAUL BRAINERD eased himself back in his chair and carefully located first one foot then the other on the corner of the desk. It was his favorite position for meditating, much to the annoyance of his wife, Ruth, who considered it undignified for a man of his calling.

"Some of my best sermons were thought out while I was in this position," he once told her in answer to a severe bout of criticism.

"That's because you rested your brains properly," she shot back.

On two sides of the mahogany paneled study row upon row of shelves stretched up from the floor. Each was amply filled with volumes of all sizes. As befitting a minister there were treatise and commentaries on Old and New Testament themes, biographies and "Selected Sermons" of famous preachers and evangelists, a large Bible Encyclopaedia set, plus various volumes on church law and government.

Competing for space was a collection of works devoted to crime and punishment. They ranged from the ponderous Snow's Criminal Code to the works of such recognized mystery authorities as Sir Arthur Conan Doyle, Raymond Chandler and Erle Stanley Gardner.

Collected over the years the library had earned Brainerd the respect and envy of many professionals and helped establish his reputation as one of the nation's foremost amateur criminologists.

His success in assisting law enforcement agencies in solving a number of celebrated cases brought him many invitations to address local bar associations and service clubs. In fact, there were nearly as many of these invitations as there were invitations to hold crusades around the country.

In his mind there was no conflict of interest. He considered this aspect of his make-up to be just as much a gift as his preaching. It permitted him to reach a segment of society with the Gospel that generally considered itself too sophisticated ever to attend an evangelistic crusade.

His knowledge about the current crime and punishment situation was remarkable. This was mainly due to an insatiable appetite for reading countless legal journals and court reports. Whenever he found something out of the ordinary he was like an addict. He never let the case rest until he was satisfied that it was solved satisfactorily and justice had been done. This led him into countless situations where he became personally involved much to the relief of some closely involved and the annoyance and consternation of others.

Since he had no official capacity beyond that of a private citizen he was careful not to overstep his bounds in relation to the responsibility and authority of the police departments. This generally assured him the co-operation of the police, though it was sometimes grudgingly given.

He didn't look up from the news clipping as his wife entered the room and said, "What have you there, another grisly case?"

"Believe it or not, it's out of the ordinary."

"You say that about them all. Now come on, supper's ready."

"Let me finish this. Aren't you curious?"

"I suppose so. You won't quit until you tell me, will you?"

"I'll let that pass for now and just consider that it was an idle remark from an unenlightened soul."

"I'm unenlightened all right and prefer it that way. Why don't you take no for an answer?" Her eyes were dancing with amusement.

"Because, my love, if I ever took no for an answer you would still be an old maid."

"Touché!"

"Come on now—listen to this."

He unfolded a newspaper clipping and began reading.

58

Before he had finished the first sentence his wife interrupted. "I'll read it myself later, just give me an outline."

"O.K., but you'll miss the significance."

"I'll take my chances. What happened?"

Brainerd cleared his throat. "It seems that there was a murder at Fairview Community Church. Someone took a strong dislike to one of the members and sent him to his reward in the choir room."

"What's so unusual about that? I can think of a number of church members who deserve to be dispatched in the choir room or any other room for that matter."

"I'll overlook your uncharitable disposition," Brainerd laughed. "The interesting thing about this case is the suspect, James Ferguson."

"Ferguson?" His wife knitted her brow. "That name rings a bell."

"It should—he was the young man who directed the young people's activities when we were at Rutherglen Bible Conference two years ago."

"Of course, I remember him now. He was the one who impressed you so greatly."

"That's right. I can't believe that he would do a thing like this. It's just not in character."

"Now don't get carried away. Have they convicted him?"

"No, he was released because of lack of evidence. According to this article he was arrested, but never brought to trial. Seems the Crown didn't have a strong enough case."

"What's happened to him?"

"He's back at Fairview. The story says that the membership met and gave him a vote of confidence."

"I'll bet it wasn't unanimous?"

"Why couldn't it be?"

"If he didn't do it, the chances are it was someone in the church. I doubt if he'd get an affirmative vote from that individual."

Brainerd pursed his lips. "That's a good point, a very good point."

"You're interested, aren't you?"

"Certainly I'm interested, and not just casually either. It disturbs me that there is a possibility of a promising young preacher's life being ruined because of circumstantial evidence. It also disturbs me that there is a chance that he really may have done it and is getting off scot free. Either way the Lord's work is suspect in the eyes of the world and I don't like it."

"Who sent you all this material anyway?"

"Doug Mullen, a policeman who worked on the case."

"How did he know you?"

"He attended one of my crusades last summer and came up and spoke to me after the meeting. In fact we got together practically every chance we could during the three days he was in town and exchanged notes on various cases that we both had worked on."

"You didn't tell me about him," Ruth said in mock annoyance.

"Just proves that I'm not perfect," he replied.

"You want to get involved, don't you?"

Brainerd leaned back and clasped his hands behind his head, "So bad I can taste it."

Ferguson sat in front of the window staring blankly out at the street. Occasionally he would look up and pass a comment to his wife, but generally said nothing. This had been the pattern for the past weeks and it was evident that he was undergoing a psychological metamorphosis. Despite all attempts of his wife and friends to snap him out of it, he continued to withdraw further and further into himself.

His work at the church was suffering. Phinnamore tried to give him every consideration, but relations between the two had become strained to the breaking point. The deterioration began the evening just before Charlie Scales was found murdered and continued at a rapid pace throughout the long and trying weeks of police investigation.

The ringing of the telephone broke into Ferguson's reverie.

"Jimmy, can you get it?" Betty called from the kitchen.

"No, you answer it."

Betty came into the living room mumbling about having all she could take and snatched up the receiver.

"Hello. Just a moment I'll see."

Ferguson pretended to act indifferent, but strained to hear every word.

"Jimmy," Betty held her hand over the mouthpiece, "it's Doris Brent. They are having a group back to their place after church Sunday evening and want us to come."

"Who's going to be there?"

Betty looked exasperated. "How do I know who's going to be there?"

"Ask her."

"I will not."

"All right then, we're not going."

Betty caught her breath. "Doris, I'm afraid that we won't be able to come. Jimmy's not feeling too good. Thanks for thinking of us, we appreciate it. Yes, perhaps next time. Good-by."

She hung up the phone and ran out of the room, tears stinging her eyes.

Doris Brent thoughtfully replaced the telephone and said, "Alton, they won't come."

"I'm not surprised. I would have been if they had."

"It's been four months since Charlie died. Surely Jimmy's getting over it by now?"

"Murdered," interjected her husband.

"I don't like that word. Anyway they never did find out who did it."

"Regardless of that it was murder and someone is guilty. That's the reason behind Jimmy's reluctance to socialize with anyone."

"He was released, they never even brought him to trial. Why is he still carrying on?"

"Circumstantial evidence, Doris. That old bit about being innocent until proven guilty might be the cornerstone of British justice, but it doesn't alter the fact that tongues wag and the harsh finger of suspicion is always pointed, guilty or innocent."

"It just doesn't seem fair. I can't believe that Jimmy did it, no matter what anyone says."

"I'm afraid that you're in the minority. I know for a fact that public opinion is strongly against him. Ever consider the possibility that he just may be guilty?"

"Don't be ridiculous."

"Well, someone did it."

"I know, but it wasn't anyone at the church."

"How can you be so sure? You women have a knack of rationalizing situations to fit your own ideas."

"It's not rationalization, Alton. It's just a woman's intuition, that's all."

Brent laughed, "You should be on the police force. The mystery would be solved in no time."

"Joke if you want, but I'm sure it was someone not even connected with Fairview. Someone like a prowler perhaps."

"Well if it gives you peace of mind to think that a stranger was responsible, more power to you. I think that there is more to this than just a straight murder and it won't be too long before it's cleared up."

"Do you know something you're not telling me?"

"No, just call it man's intuition." Brent picked up the book he was reading. The subject was closed as far as he was concerned.

Dick Hart went out of Phinnamore's study and came back in carrying a straight-backed Sunday school chair.

"That's what happens when you're late, you get the hardest chair," he said to Alan Hayes.

"Beats standing," replied Hayes as he moved it back closer to the wall so he could lean his head against it.

Phinnamore got up from behind his desk and motioned to Hart, "Take my chair, Dick, you're the council chairman."

Hart shrugged his shoulders and exchanged places. Before he spoke he looked around the room at those who were present. Harry Boland was sniffing the ever present inhalant, Alan Hayes stared blankly into space, Steve Gordon fidgeted with a key ring, keys rattling one against the other, and Alton Brent indifferently passed time by leafing through a book from Phinnamore's library. And Jimmy Ferguson sat quietly at one side. The men sat opposite each other, but at an angle where their eyes would not meet.

"Well I guess we're all here now," said Hart.

"All but Charlie," replied Boland.

"That's in very poor taste," remarked Brent without looking up. Boland glared!

Hart cleared his throat. "I suppose that we had better get on with this meeting," he began. "If you all have read the agenda you will realize that this meeting has been called to consider the possibility of holding an evangelistic crusade in the church next summer. We will have to decide on who we are going to invite and what the dates will be, also make some firm plans as to publicity."

Brent uncrossed his legs. "You haven't listed the proposed speakers. Who are they?"

"I'll get around to that in a moment, Alt. First, are there any objections to this suggestion? What about you, pastor?"

Phinnamore rubbed his chin. "I think it is an ideal plan. When I heard about it I immediately thought that if it could be arranged it might be interesting to hold it in the form of an old-time camp meeting. Perhaps even erect a tent in the parking lot. The older members would like it, I'm sure, and the younger ones would come if only out of curiosity."

"Hoy, that's a good idea," said Boland. "I like it."

Hart tapped his pencil on the desk. "You'll all get a chance to offer your opinions, one at a time. Now then, I think we should have a motion to that effect."

Boland raised his hand, "I'll move it."

Gordon nodded his head.

"You seconding it, Steve?"

"Yes."

"All right then, all in favor? Carried. Now let's decide on the date, then on who we should ask," said Hart.

For the next fifteen to twenty minutes various dates were suggested and rejected for one reason or another. Finally, a compromise was made and it was agreed to hold a ten-day crusade finishing up on the Labor Day weekend in September.

Phinnamore and Ferguson had refrained from entering into the discussion with the exception of Phinnamore's suggestion about holding the crusade in the form of a camp meeting. Ferguson remained morose throughout the evening. At previous meetings he joked with those in attendance, especially Gordon, but this time he only answered in monosyllabic grunts. It was uncomfortably evident to those there that he couldn't care less. Hart tried to draw him into the conversation on a couple of occasions, but was openly rebuffed for his efforts so left him alone.

"Sounds like a great thing for the church. It'll certainly start the fall work off with a bang," observed Boland. "Now all we have to do is line up a topnotch speaker and some good music."

"That's just what I was coming to. I have a couple of names to put forth. If you have anyone in mind speak up, this is an open meeting as far as that goes."

The discussion that followed centered around the names suggested by Hart. Each one was thoroughly considered but rejected for one reason or another. When the list was depleted Hart suggested that they go home and give it some thought and come back with more names in a week.

Brent reached inside his coat pocket and took out a brochure. "Before we give up I have one name that hasn't been mentioned."

"Speak up, man," said Hayes.

Brent unfolded the brochure. "A couple of summers ago when Doris and I were on holidays we attended an evangelistic crusade and were so impressed by the speaker that I made a point of talking to him after the meeting and getting some literature on his work. This brochure explains everything. If no one has any objections I move that we issue him an invitation to be our guest evangelist."

Everyone crowded around Brent as he laid out the brochure on the desk, with the exception of Ferguson who hung back from the rest.

"You really think he's a good man do you, Alt?" asked Hayes.

"Yes, it's been a long time since I've heard a speaker who could move a congregation the way this man did. The response following the sermon was unbelievable."

"All right then, I'll second the motion."

Hart looked at the faces of the other men. "All in favor, contrary, carried. I'll write a formal letter inviting him to hold a ten-day evangelistic crusade on the dates agreed upon. I'll let you all know his answer as soon as I receive a reply. This meeting is adjourned."

As they started to leave the room Boland remarked to no one in particular, "I think I'm going to like this man. Even his name has a good ring . . . Paul Brainerd!"

Chapter 10

BETTY FERGUSON FIDGETED nervously with the handle of her purse. Each time the telephone rang she inwardly jumped. There was a time when she would have found a police station fascinating, but no more. The constant stream of misery passing the bench on which she sat only increased her anxiety. Before, she would have viewed each one with objective interest, now she felt she was one of them. It was a constant struggle for her to keep fighting back the panic of not knowing for sure whether or not the next twenty-four hours would climax in her world being shattered.

Across the room she heard an intercom buzzing and the sergeant saying, "Yes sir, she's right here. I'll bring her up."

Instead of leaning over the counter and calling instructions to her as he had with so many others the officer walked out of the enclosure and over to where she sat.

"Mrs. Ferguson, Inspector Potter will see you now. Will you please come with me?"

"Thank you, I know where his office is."

"That's all right, Mrs. Ferguson, I'll be pleased to show you the way."

As they reached the elevator it suddenly opened and out poured two scruffy men handcuffed together and in the custody of a burly constable. They purposely had their heads down and barged right at Betty.

"Just a moment, you two, where are your manners? Step aside and let the lady past." The officer jerked one of the men sharply by the arm.

"Whatch'a in for, beautiful?" sneered the dirtiest looking one.

"Quiet!" ordered the policeman and received a sullen snort for his trouble.

"Sorry about that, ma'am, some people just have no sense of respect."

"It's all right, officer, I don't mind."

When they reached the door with Potter's name in gold-leaf on it, the officer gently tapped.

"Come in."

"Go right ahead, Mrs. Ferguson."

"Thank you."

Potter was seated at his desk and rose when he saw Betty enter.

"Come right in, thank you so much for coming. I hope I didn't keep you waiting too long?"

"No, it's quite all right."

Potter shuffled the papers on his desk into a neat pile.

"Now, then, I'll try not to take up too much of your time so will come directly to the point. How has your husband been since the inquest?"

"Just awful. I think he's going out of his mind."

Potter looked thoughtfully out the window. "What makes you think that?"

"Well," her voice wavered, "he won't talk, go out, or see anyone, especially anyone from the church."

"I can understand that. After all, he's been through quite an experience for a young man."

"You don't think he had anything to do with the murder, do you?" Betty looked pleadingly into the eyes of the older man.

"He was released—we've no reason to hold him."

"You didn't answer me. You must have thought he was innocent or why would you let him go?"

"Mrs. Ferguson," Potter's voice was quietly confident, "I'm paid by the authorities to clear up matters like this. Up to now we've been batting our head against a brick wall. In fact, I've always felt that this case was hanging together by a brittle thread. Now thankfully, that thread has been reinforced. That's why I've asked you to come in today and have a talk. I need your help."

"My help, what can I do?"

"You want to help your husband and have his name cleared, don't you?"

"Oh yes, he can't stand much more."

"Fine, I knew I could count on you."

"What do you want me to do?"

"Help your husband have a nervous breakdown!"

Paul Brainerd was ecstatic. It would have been difficult for him to single out which pleased him the most: the crusade at Fairview or the prospects of possibly being involved in the mystery which surrounded the church.

He had his letter of acceptance written and in the very next mail. The suggestion that the crusade be held in the form of an old-time camp meeting pleased him. From his knowledge of Fairview and its problems he thought that it was an excellent idea since it would move the congregation out of the church and onto relatively neutral ground.

Doug Mullen had kept Brainerd abreast as well as he could of all the happenings concerning the unsolved murder. Once he had accepted the invitation Brainerd immediately wrote Mullen and asked him if he could supply more information, in detail. Much to his surprise Mullen not only replied with a sheaf of documents, he even suggested that his superior, Inspector Potter, would be pleased to personally meet with him during his stay at Fairview.

The Central Police Station was a forbidding limestone relic from out of the last century. Outside it looked almost archaic—inside it presented an air of scientific efficiency. For many years the police had worked under cramped conditions in poorly lit rooms, but all that had changed. Following the election of a new mayor and board of control, money was allocated for a complete remodeling and refurnishing program for the building. There was a stipulation, however—the exterior had to remain untouched because of its historic value.

Brainerd was immediately impressed with the interior. He had seen the inside of police bureaus across the country and this, he thought, ranked with the best.

"May I help you, sir?" asked the officer behind the desk.

"Yes, I'd like to see Sergeant of Detectives Mullen, please?"

"Is he expecting you?"

"Yes."

"Who shall I say is calling?"

"Paul Brainerd."

The officer pushed a button on a large switchboard console and said, "Sergeant, there's a Mr. Paul Brainerd here to see you."

"He'll be right down, sir."

"Thank you."

In a moment Brainerd could hear the clicking of feet coming down the hall and from behind the outstretched hand was a massive grinning face.

"Paul, it's good to see you."

"Hello, Doug."

The two men shook hands warmly.

"Come on up to my office, we can talk there," said Mullen as he guided Brainerd to the elevator.

Over coffee the two friends brought one another up-to-date on what they had been doing. Brainerd could hardly contain himself, he was itching to get the subject around to Fairview.

"Now that we've got the pleasantries over," he laughed, "let's get down to the real reason why I'm here."

"Fairview?"

"Exactly, Doug, Fairview. What's happened since you sent me all the material?"

Mullen reached over and picked up the telephone.

"Is Inspector Potter there?"

"Mullen, Inspector. Paul Brainerd is with me now. Thanks, we'll be right over."

As they hurried down the long corridor to Potter's office Brainerd felt a surge of excitement. The same exhilaration he experienced any time he preached a particularly powerful sermon and saw the people moved to respond.

Potter had the ever-present pipe clenched between his teeth. After Mullen had made the introductions the three men sat around a large table which was strewn with pictures and papers.

"I thought that you might be interested in seeing the case from the time we were called in, so I dug up everything I could find," said Potter. "When Doug told me that you were coming to Fairview for some meetings I was delighted. I heard you a couple of years ago at a police convention and have followed your career with interest ever since. There's hardly an issue of the police journal that doesn't mention you in some way or another."

"That's very kind of you."

"Not at all. I'm a busy man and have no time for crackpots or amateur Sam Spades. I wouldn't be bothered with you either except that you have turned a hobby into a useful avocation. You also know how to approach the police and that's important. You know we're not the stupid clods that television sometimes pictures us to be."

Brainerd laughed. "I've always made a point of emphasizing that whenever I speak."

"Yes, I know," replied Potter. "If you tried to overstep your limited authority you would be on the outside looking in, believe me. Now that we've finished congratulating ourselves let's get down to business. I think that you can play a vital role in clearing up this situation. Interested?"

"You bet I am. What do you have in mind?"

Potter tapped out his pipe and began refilling it. "I have never met a more closed mouth group of individuals before in my life than that crowd at Fairview. They tell me exactly what they want to tell me and no more. There's one especially, Gordon, that just about drove me up the wall. I can't figure the guy out. I want you to see what you can turn up from the inside. Know what I mean?"

"Yes. How far do you want me to go?"

"Right to a conviction if possible."

"How much time do I have?"

"How much can you spare?"

Brainerd took out a pocket diary and leafed through the pages. "I'm clear for the next three weeks and could possibly arrange my schedule for another week or so if necessary."

"Fine, I don't think it will take nearly that long. I've been working on a plan for a few weeks and it's starting to take shape."

"Do you have an idea who did it?"

"Yes and no. As you probably know I pulled in James Ferguson early in the case and went through the motions of holding him for the inquest. It sure stirred up the congregation at Fairview."

"You obviously don't think he had anything to do with it then?"

"No, Paul, he's clean." Potter stopped abruptly. "You don't mind me calling you Paul do you?"

"Not at all."

Potter's eyes twinkled. "I can call you Paul and Mullen here Doug, but you both have to call me Inspector. Right, Doug?"

"Right, Inspector," replied Mullen with mock respect.

Potter tamped down the tobacco in his pipe and struck a match. "Ferguson is going through quite a time. He's still very much suspect by many at Fairview and I'm doing my best to keep the pot boiling. If I can keep the attention of everyone on him it will give the one I'm after ample opportunity to feel over-confident and make a mistake. This is where you come in. I want to know what really is behind the murder. All I can find out so far is a jumbled mess of truths and half-truths."

"You said you had a plan. Can you tell me what it is?"

"I was going to get around to it. Doug here has been more or less working on the inside. For the past couple of months he's been attending the services at Fairview and has been reasonably accepted into the outer fringes of the membership."

"Don't they connect him with the investigation?"

"Not especially. One or two asked him about it, but generally speaking they just look upon him as someone who's searching for the truth and light."

Mullen chuckled, "I'm searching for the truth all right."

"Found out much, Doug?" asked Brainerd.

"Enough to know that there's something going on. I can't put my finger on it because no one will really open up. I think they're still uneasy about me."

Potter slapped the desk with his hand. "That's the whole point of asking you to help, Paul. We can't reach these people, but I think you could."

Brainerd stood up. "All right, I'll do what I can. I have two reasons for getting involved. One, I don't like to see a kid like Ferguson nailed, and two, I'm a minister of the Gospel and I don't appreciate seeing a church which has been so prominent reduced to a curiosity piece in the community. Its ministry is useless when it only fills the auditorium with thrill-seekers instead of Christ-seekers."

"Those are honest reasons, Paul. Something akin to mine. Now then let's get working. You have a lot of homework to do because I want you as familiar with the case as I am. I know what material Doug sent you so we won't waste time on it."

Potter rummaged through a file on his desk and pulled out a yellow piece of paper. "What do you know about Harrison Phinnamore, Paul?"

"Not too much except that he's well respected in church circles."

"What about his wife?"

"I've only met her once and that was a year or so ago at a missionary convention. She appeared to be a very gracious woman, the perfect minister's wife. Why?"

"Take a look at this." Potter handed the paper across the table.

Brainerd studied it and knitted his brow.

"Any chance of a mistake?"

"That's the first thing I want you to find out!"

Chapter 11

DICK HART SPEARHEADED the "Brainerd Crusade" publicity committee. He met with Brainerd two months in advance of the meetings and worked out a mutually satisfactory schedule for promotion and publicity which included: advertising; posters; personal visitation throughout the community; cottage prayer meetings and feature stories highlighting the camp meeting theme in the religious and news pages of local newspapers. There were interviews with senior citizens in the church who remembered the camp meetings of their youth which made good human interest copy.

The results of this activity brought a refreshing air of excitement and anticipation into the church. The "Scales Affair," as it had become known, was thankfully pushed into the background and hardly ever mentioned. Occasionally, someone would wonder out loud about the murder and who was responsible, but they were quickly squelched by a sharp retort or withering look.

Phinnamore was coming out of his shell and taking hold of the work. The relationship between him and his assistant had modified and by gentle persuasion he had been able to involve Ferguson once again. Since Jim had the advantage of working with Brainerd in the past, it was decided that his assignment would be the young people. Phinnamore refrained from issuing specific instructions. Rather he suggested that Ferguson use his own judgment and do whatever was necessary to gain the support and enthusiasm of this vital group for the crusade.

Betty welcomed the challenge for her husband. His attitude had deteriorated and was far from healthy. Ever since she had met with

73

Potter her attitude had changed drastically also. Instead of the docile, understanding wife she had become demanding and relentless. For quite some time Ferguson had taken to leaving the house without any explanation and returning at odd hours. When questioned he simply remained silent and would only say that "his business was his affair and he had to have some life to himself."

In the beginning Betty would accept this but no longer. There was one explosive scene when they argued far into the early morning. Ferguson had returned after one of his extended absences, brushed aside her demands and went to bed. When his wife turned on the light she was shocked to see his appearance. His face was pallid and his eyes glazed. He assured her that he hadn't been drinking. She accepted this mainly because she could not bring herself to believe that he had been indulging. The only other answer was drugs and this deeply concerned her, possibly more than if he had been drinking.

Their circle of friends had completely vanished. They had refused so many invitations that people just stopped asking. Even the Gordons had ceased from making overtures of friendship. Ferguson told her it was because he was still the prime suspect in many eyes and they were just waiting until the long arm of the law reached out and pulled him in. Betty called Muriel Gordon on a few occasions, but the conversation, while polite, was strained. It was not her nature to push herself onto someone when she felt that she was not wanted, so she stopped calling.

It was a beautiful summer evening. A cool breeze cut through the heat of the afternoon and veranda after veranda was filled with people either rocking back and forth or just lounging, enjoying the blessed relief from the heat and humidity.

The front door of the Ferguson home opened and a man appeared, letting the screen door slam behind him. For a moment he just stood with his hands thrust deep into his pockets. From behind the screen the figure of a woman could be made out.

"Jimmy!"

"What?"

"Do you have to go out again tonight?"

"I thought we were all through that at supper! Yes I'm going out. No, I don't know when I'll be home. Get off my back, will you?"

"Have fun, because I won't be here when you get back," shouted the woman as she slammed the front door. Heads, up and down the street, turned toward the Ferguson house as the slamming door boomed like a cannon in the stillness of the night.

Ferguson stood still for a moment, then got in his car and screeched the tires as he roared down the street.

Inside, Betty leaned against the wall of the vestibule and caught her breath. This was the worst yet. Tears streamed down her cheeks in rivulets as she fought for control. In the semi-darkness of the evening she stumbled into the living room and slumped into the large easy chair, Jimmy's favorite chair, and buried her face in her hands.

She lost all track of time and woke with a start as lights from a car grazed the front windows. She leaped to her feet and running to the door threw it open.

"Jimmy, thank God you've come back."

Instead of her husband it was a man with a suitcase who said, "I'm sorry, I'm not Jimmy. My name's Paul Brainerd. Dick Hart said I'd be staying with you and your husband. It's Betty Ferguson, isn't it?"

Betty wiped her eyes with her apron. "Yes, I'm Betty, won't you please come in?"

"Thank you, I'll just be a moment. I have to pay the cab driver."

Brainerd returned quickly and followed Betty into the living room.

"I'm so sorry, I didn't mean to embarrass you. I thought you were Jimmy, I. . . ."

Brainerd held up his hand, "Think nothing of it, Betty. I may call you Betty, may I?"

"Yes, of course, but I do want to explain."

"No explanations are necessary. I understand perfectly."

"You don't understand, no one understands," she burst into tears.

Brainerd waited patiently for her to stop, then handed her a large white handkerchief.

"Feel better now?"

"Yes, I suppose so." Betty wiped her eyes which had become puffy and red from crying.

"I must look a mess. What will you think?"

"I'll think that I've found a wife like my Ruth who worries about her husband, that's what I'll think."

"If your wife's like me I pity her," replied Betty with a slight edge to her voice.

"Why do you pity her? I think it's an admirable quality."

"Well, that's your opinion. Would you like to have a cup of tea? I need something."

Brainerd laughed and followed her into the kitchen.

"You're a guest, let me bring it into the living room."

"I'd rather have it in the kitchen if it's all right with you. All we ministers ever see are living rooms. Personally I like to relax and the kitchen is one of the best places to do it. Besides, my mother once said that a good way to know what a woman is like is to see her in the kitchen."

Betty looked around at the dirty dishes and pots. "You must have a good impression of me then. Just look at this mess, it's like a pig pen."

Brainerd got up from the table. "Why don't you let me help you clean up? Then we can sit and chat until Jimmy arrives."

"It'll be a long chat, he probably won't be home till morning . . . if then."

Betty looked at the clock. "It's after three. Where on earth can he be?"

"Don't worry, he'll be along," replied Brainerd. "How about some more tea?"

Before Betty could reach the stove the front door opened quietly and Ferguson crept into the hall. When he saw the light on in the kitchen he tried to peer through the semi-darkness.

"Is that you, Betty?"

"Yes, who did you think it was?" Her voice appeared to have the same harsh edge as it had when they last parted.

76

Ferguson sighed and started up the stairs, but stopped when he saw Betty in the kitchen door.

"I'm not finished, Jimmy."

"Well, I am, so you might as well give up. I'm not going to argue."

"Come into the kitchen," Betty commanded.

"Look, I'm tired, can't it wait?"

"No it can't, I want you to come into the kitchen."

Ferguson knew that from the sound of her voice he had better give in and do what she wanted. With dragging feet he retraced his steps down the stairs and followed his wife through the kitchen door. Once he reached the brightly lit room a firm hand grabbed his shoulder and spun him around.

"What the. . . ."

"Hello Jimmy, good to see you."

"Paul, Paul Brainerd, when did you get here? Hart told me to expect you tomorrow or the next day."

"Don't always keep to schedule. You should remember that from when we worked together."

Betty slipped her hand into Jimmy's and beamed up at him. "Paul told me everything. Why couldn't you have told me? It would have been so much easier."

"Told you what? What's going on here?"

"Sit down, Jimmy. I'm working with Inspector Potter and I know all about your little charade," said Brainerd.

Ferguson looked at them both, reluctant to give anything away.

"Come on, Jimmy, sit down," commanded Brainerd. "I'll tell you everything I know, then you can tell me if I'm right or not. O.K?"

Ferguson eased himself into a kitchen chair and stared across the table at Brainerd.

"You're out of your mind, completely mad, the both of you."

"We're not mad, Jimmy. You're supposed to be though," said Betty as she squeezed his hand. "Here, drink this, you'll feel better." She placed a full cup of tea in front of him.

Ferguson took a couple of refreshing gulps and put the cup down. "Now will you please explain just what you're trying to get at?"

"All right, Jimmy, here it is." Brainerd suddenly looked all business. He was deadly serious. "Inspector Potter asked me to work on the Scales murder after he heard I would be at Fairview holding a crusade. As you know, criminology has been a hobby of mine for many years and in certain circles I'm considered somewhat of an authority on the subject. I usually make it a practice of not becoming involved with people I know, something similar to a doctor not treating members of his own family. This case is different. First, I think I know you and never for a moment believed that you were involved despite the heavy circumstantial evidence. Secondly, as I've explained to Potter, I don't like the House of God being used as a slaughter house and then being turned into a three-ring circus. Follow me so far?"

Ferguson took another drink of tea and nodded his head.

"Fine, let's go on. This case has some remarkable features about it that sets it aside from any other that I've ever come in contact with. The complete lack of suspects is peculiar. That frankly is the main reason why Potter has had to rely on people like you and Betty for setting the stage. If you remember your Shakespeare you'll see the comparison. Hamlet suspected Claudius in the death of his father, but he couldn't prove it until he devised the idea of trapping Claudius by a ruse. He had some actors put on a play in which they acted out a situation which paralleled his idea of the murder. While Claudius watched the play, Hamlet and Horatio watched Claudius, waiting for him to make a slip. In other words, as Hamlet put it, 'The play's the thing wherein I'll catch the conscience of the King.' "

Ferguson looked puzzled. "You lost me. What's Hamlet got to do with us?"

Betty threw up her hands in exasperation. "Don't be so thick, honey. We're the players."

"That's right, Jimmy. You and Betty are the players, I'm Horatio and Potter's Hamlet!"

"Who's Claudius?" asked Ferguson.

"Yes, who's Claudius? That's where Shakespeare had the advantage over us. He knew who the murderer was all along and left it up to Hamlet to find out. We haven't finished casting our production yet. The starring role is still open." Brainerd rubbed his hands.

Brainerd drummed his fingers impatiently on the side of the telephone. If he had any shortcomings it was his dislike of anything mechanical which he couldn't control. Vending machines, which don't return goods, automatic doors, which don't open and especially telephones which are not answered by the third ring, were his pet peeves. His irritation was steadily mounting when the metallic click on the other end of the line indicated that the call had been completed.

"Hello."

"Inspector, it's Paul."

"Yes, Paul, sorry I took so long to answer, I was down the hall."

"I was beginning to wonder if I'd missed you."

"No, I'll always be available at ten in the morning, if not I'll have Doug cover for me."

"Can't I ever use the station number?"

"Not unless you're in a real spot. I don't want any record of your calls. That's why I gave you my private number. Now then, how are you making out?"

"Not bad. I got the Fergusons straightened out. It was a good idea. I don't think they would have held together very much longer!"

"Fine, are they going to continue?"

"Yes, and I think they'll be even better."

"Good. Did you explain everything?"

"Practically. I did what you told me and set them up for the final act."

Potter's voice faded for a moment and he could hear him talking to someone. "Doug wants to know if they've received any more phone calls?"

"Jimmy didn't say so but Betty thought there might have been one but she wasn't sure. It could have been a wrong number. Why?"

"I hope they don't stop altogether. As long as our friend keeps making them we have a good indication that he's not flown the coop. Say, did Ferguson explain his appearance? I told him to tell his wife if she pushed too far or was going to break."

"Yes, that's about the first thing she asked after I explained that both of them were working for you without the other knowing. Jimmy told her that the police doctor had given him some diet pills which were really amphetamines and drastically affected his appearance once the stimulation wore off. After she realized he hadn't been drinking she said that he could use some diet pills."

"Sounds like that situation has been taken care of. I still want those two to carry on as they have been, even more so if possible."

"They will. I gave them a few suggestions that should really keep things moving."

"Can you contact Phinnamore and see if there's anything to the report?"

"Yes, I've already called them and they invited me over to dinner."

"Play it cool, Paul. I think we're on to something. I'd follow this up myself except that they'll give you more right now than they would me. I'll have Doug get the information to you. Where are you now?"

"Just a moment." Brainerd stepped out of the telephone booth and looked at the street signs on the corner. "I'm in a phone booth at the north-east corner of Inverleigh and Forest Hill Road."

"O.K. stay there. Doug's leaving right now."

Brainerd shifted the receiver to his other ear. "Are you sure you're on the right track?"

"I hope so. I've got no other choice."

"What if it backfires?"

"You're a minister. Just pray that it doesn't."

Chapter 12

THERE WAS NOTHING Harry Boland hated more than the last three weeks of August and the first four or five in September. For anyone with allergies, the hay fever season is pure torture. As the pollen count mounted so did Boland's discomfort. With the aid of anti-histamines, however, he was able to control the problem to some degree. His voice, while naturally deep and husky, took on added properties as the season approached and at times was nothing more than a deep-chested wheeze.

Since he had to be careful to regulate the amount of drug intake his only comfort was an inhalant which had become his constant companion during the day and a portable humidifier at night. Difficult as it was for him, it was probably more so for his family who had to put up with his sneezing and jarring gasps for breath.

"Harry, can't you do that somewhere else?" asked his distraught wife.

"Do what?"

"All that doctoring. I swear, if I hear you sniffing once more today I'll go out of my mind."

Boland didn't answer her. Instead he picked up all his medicines and equipment and, mumbling to himself, shuffled out of the kitchen and upstairs.

As he reached the landing the door bell rang. He was about to answer it when his wife came out of the dining room and said, "Go on, you'd die before you got to it."

She could see the dark form of a man through the glass.

"Yes?" she said as she partly opened the door.

"Is Mr. Boland in?"

"Yes, won't you come in?"

"Thank you," said the man as he stepped into the vestibule.

"Harry, there's someone to see you," called his wife.

"I don't believe we have met yet, Mrs. Boland. I'm Paul Brainerd."

Mrs. Boland wiped her hands on the front of her apron and fussed with her hair. "Reverend Brainerd, I'm sorry I didn't recognize you, do come in. Harry, it's Reverend Brainerd."

"That's quite all right, Mrs. Boland. I'm just making a few calls before the crusade starts."

Boland came downstairs and placed his bottles and equipment on the hall table and took the outstretched hand.

"It's so good to meet you. We're all looking forward to your meetings."

"Thank you, you're very kind."

"Harry, where are your manners? Take Reverend Brainerd into the living room." The command was punctuated by a sharp elbow in Boland's ribs.

Over tea and cake Brainerd was able to expertly maneuver the conversation around to Scales and the events of his death.

"I suppose you heard all about the unfortunate accident in the church, Reverend?" asked Mrs. Boland.

"Well, yes I did, but I really haven't heard two stories which agreed."

Boland put his cup down on the coffee table with a thud. "If you would like to hear what really happened I'll tell you."

"Now, Harry, don't get riled up," said his wife.

"You just leave me be. I haven't talked about it for some time now."

"Must be all of a day," she interjected.

Boland looked at her out of the corner of his eye while Brainerd grinned.

"I think that I probably know as much about it as anybody. After all I'm a prime witness." Boland stiffened his shoulders and threw his head back in obvious pride.

Skillfully Brainerd drew him out. "When did you become involved?"

"Probably right after poor Charlie was done in. I was driving by the church and saw Jimmy Ferguson running out the back door. I'll bet he had just finished killing Charlie."

"How can you be sure?"

"Instinct, Reverend, instinct, I. . . ." Boland turned his head to the side and pulled out a large handkerchief just before his whole body convulsed in a sneeze.

"Watch out, Reverend, you'll get killed if you get in the way," cautioned Mrs. Boland.

"Sorry, Reverend, I suffer from allergies."

"So I see," replied Brainerd.

"Where were we? Oh yes. I told the coroner's inquest that I was sure Ferguson did it, but they wouldn't listen to me. They let him go."

"Evidently they felt there wasn't sufficient evidence to warrant holding him for trial."

"They don't know what they're doing. Have you heard what he's been like since the inquest?"

"Not really. As I said, I've heard a number of things."

"Guilty as sin. I've never seen anyone so guilty in all my life. You know what?" He didn't wait for Brainerd to reply. "Even his wife has her doubts. I hear they're having trouble. It all stems from him not being positively cleared. What do you think of that?"

Brainerd was pensive. "I can't believe that a man wouldn't be given the benefit of a doubt, particularly in Christian circles. Do you honestly think that just seeing a man run out of a building is grounds for a conviction, especially in something so serious as murder?"

Boland warmed up. "That's just part of it. I hope you don't think I'd condemn a man on something that flimsy, do you? After all, I'm a Christian and have charity in my heart."

"Not at all, Mr. Boland, I'm pleased to hear you say that. It's reassuring."

"I should say so. The thing that really clinches it in my mind is his motive."

Brainerd had finally reached his man and knew it. "From what I've heard there hasn't been a motive established and that's what has the police baffled."

"It's as plain as the nose on your face—jealousy, pure and simple. Ferguson was jealous of Pastor Phinnamore and wanted the pulpit at Fairview."

Brainerd looked blank. "I'm afraid you lost me somewhere. How would the murder of a man like Mr. Scales get him the pastorate of the church?"

Boland looked aghast. "Don't you see? If he could cast suspicion on the pastor it would give him clear sailing. I had it figured out the day after the murder."

"How would he do that? They were friends, weren't they?"

Boland looked self-confident. "That's what everyone thought. Ferguson's skillful and tricky. Lies through his teeth. Know what he told one of the council members?"

"No, what?"

Boland leaned over to Brainerd and lowered his voice. "He told this man that Pastor Phinnamore was at the church with him the night Charlie was killed. Now what do you think of that?"

"What does Reverend Phinnamore say?"

"Nothing. No one that heard Ferguson's story has approached the pastor. As far as I know only this man and I know about it. After all, don't you think the pastor would tell the police if that was the case?"

"You'd think so, wouldn't you?" replied Brainerd.

"You bet you would. That's not all. Why I know enough to put Ferguson on the gallows. I'm a student of crime and punishment you know."

"I can see you are. Don't you think that the police would be interested in your information?"

"Let them solve it themselves. I tried to help Inspector Potter but all I got for my trouble was a dressing down."

"What for?"

Boland shuffled uncomfortably in his chair. "Just because I saw it for what it was and called it murder. That's all."

Brainerd had learned what he wanted to and rose to his feet.

"Mrs. Boland, the refreshments were delicious. Thank you so much." He stretched out his hand toward Boland. "Thank you for filling me in. I have a much better picture of what really happened. It'll help me when the crusade starts. Always better to know one's ground."

"I hope we have the pleasure of another visit before you leave, Reverend," smiled Mrs. Boland.

"I'd look forward to that," replied Brainerd.

As they walked to the front door Boland chatted about the need in church of a spiritual awakening. Brainerd nodded his head in apparent agreement and stepped out onto the veranda.

"Who did you say Ferguson told about the pastor being with him on the night of the murder?" he asked, turning to face the Bolands.

Boland looked deep into Brainerd's eyes. "One of the most respected men in the church, Steve Gordon. Why?"

Brainerd shrugged his shoulders. "No reason, just curious."

Boland followed him out onto the veranda. "I have an idea. Why don't you ask Steve yourself if you're so interested? He'll tell you."

Brainerd waved his hand as he left the steps. "I may just do that. Thanks for the suggestion."

Beth Phinnamore was everything a minister's wife should be. She was gracious, gentle and the perfect hostess. The dinner was superb. Brainerd found it a joy to sit back and watch this expert perform in her own surroundings.

The dinner table conversation ranged from light-hearted comments about the weather and favorite vacation spots to involved discussions about philosophical and Biblical points of view.

Brainerd was pleased to see that Phinnamore welcomed his wife's comments, even encouraged them. It was a refreshing departure from many of his colleagues who viewed their wife's place as in the kitchen with conversation to suit.

"Would you two like to move into the living room while I clear off the table?" asked Mrs. Phinnamore.

"Why don't you leave the dishes and join us?" replied her husband.

"They'll only take a moment. I don't like the looks of a table after dinner. Somehow it appears like a battleground after the armies have withdrawn. Don't you think so, Reverend Brainerd?"

"That's the first time I've heard it put just like that, Mrs. Phinnamore, but you're so right," smiled Brainerd.

After the two men were comfortably seated in big high-backed chairs Phinnamore's face became grave.

"I suppose that you have been well primed about what happened at the church?"

"Yes, I've had a number of people attempt to fill me in."

"It's terrible, just terrible. I really don't know how it's all going to end. You know, I've thought about resigning many times during the last couple of years. Sometimes I think I made a mistake in carrying on. Perhaps things would have been different if I'd had the courage to do it."

"Why do you think that?"

"There are a number of reasons. I think I've lost touch with my people and sometimes I even think I've lost touch with God. Can you imagine it? After all these years they didn't trust me enough to come right out and ask me if I wanted an assistant. They had to be devious and so formal."

"Didn't you want one?"

"Yes, I wanted one. As a matter of fact I had thought about approaching the council with the idea long before they brought it up."

"Why didn't you tell them that?"

"What good would it have done?"

Mrs. Phinnamore started to walk into the room but stopped when she saw the two men in deep conversation.

Phinnamore looked up. "Come on in, Beth, we're just chatting."

"No, you two enjoy your talk. You don't want a woman butting in."

Brainerd had risen to his feet when he saw Mrs. Phinnamore. "Please stay. You contribute so much to the conversation."

"I'll join you both later. It was nice of you to ask." She turned around and left the room.

Brainerd sat down and fixed his eyes on the older man.

"You haven't an easy congregation to preach to. I don't envy you," said Phinnamore.

"I don't mind. In fact I look forward to the challenge. What would be the use of preaching to a church full of saints? That's not my ministry. I leave that type of preaching up to giants of the faith like you."

Phinnamore laughed to himself. "Giants like me. If I was so great you wouldn't have been asked. Do you really know why they asked you?"

"No, why?"

"Because neither Jimmy nor I can move these people in any way, shape or form. Frankly, I'm convinced that our days here at Fairview are numbered. I dare say that we won't have the option of deciding whether or not we want to resign. The decision will be made for us."

"Oh, come now. Don't you think that's putting it a little strongly?"

"No I don't. After all, the murder is still unsolved and everyone is under suspicion, especially Jimmy."

"Yes, I understand that he hasn't satisfactorily cleared himself."

"Who told you that?"

"Harry Boland. I had a talk with him."

"Harry Boland. I might have guessed. That man can't keep his mouth shut or his ideas to himself. He's to blame for more unrest in the church than any other person since the unpleasantness."

"He seemed to think he knows the solution."

"Does he now? And just what does he think it is?"

Brainerd tried to look uncomfortable. Phinnamore was beginning to open up and he didn't want to upset the mood. "Well, he thinks Jimmy is guilty."

"Oh," replied Phinnamore. "That's not news, he's said that ever since the murder. What else did he say?"

"Well, he implied that Jimmy was jealous of you and wanted the church. He said that by casting suspicion on you it would keep it off himself."

87

"How could he do that? Jimmy has never said anything detrimental that I've heard."

"Have you talked with a Steve Gordon?"

"What's Gordon got to do with it?"

"Jimmy and he were great friends, weren't they?"

"Yes, but I guess Jimmy's overall attitude finished that relationship. I once asked Gordon what had happened between them, but he wouldn't say."

"That's strange," said Brainerd. "Boland said that Jimmy still confides in Gordon. In fact, according to Gordon, he is supposed to have said that you were with him at the church the night before Scales was found."

There was a noticeable change in Phinnamore's appearance. He thrust forward in the chair, then relaxed. "That's utter nonsense— they aren't even speaking to each other. Anyway, don't you think I'd have said I was?"

"That's what Boland said. He's very loyal to you. So loyal in fact, that he never even repeated what he'd heard to anyone. He probably wonders why he even told me."

"Boland's a fool!" spat Phinnamore.

Brainerd leaned forward in his chair. "You weren't with him, were you?"

"I just said it was nonsense, didn't I? If I had been with Jimmy don't you think he would have told the police instead of giving them some lame excuse which couldn't be collaborated?"

Brainerd looked away, apparently in deep thought. "I asked Jimmy that very question last night."

"What did he say?"

"Nothing, except I had the feeling he was either trying to hide something or protect someone, perhaps both."

Phinnamore became restless and got up from where he was seated. "Say, what's your real interest in this matter?"

Brainerd was off-handed. "Nothing in particular. It's no secret that I'm interested in mysteries. I find this one fascinating. Hope you don't object?"

Phinnamore returned to his chair. "No, I don't care, except that you puzzle me."

"How's that?"

"You're so well informed, and in such a short space of time. Here you are, in town just a few hours and already conducting an investigation like you were working for the police or something. It's beyond me."

"I'm not trying to be mysterious or anything," assured Brainerd. "I knew all about the case long before I was ever invited to hold the crusade. Since I'm interested in this type of thing I make it a point to know what's happening. I was more interested in this one because I knew Jimmy and found it hard to believe that he would be mixed up in something like this."

"Well, I suppose so," replied Phinnamore. "I've long since ceased to question anyone's motives."

Brainerd wanted to keep Phinnamore talking. He felt he was close to a breakthrough and was firmly convinced, as was Potter, that this man held the key to the murder. "Let's change the subject shall we? I'd like to hear about your early ministry."

Phinnamore looked relieved. "Thanks, I'm getting sick and tired of the whole thing. What would you like to know? I'm a very simple person who once thought that being a minister of the Gospel was the finest calling a man could have."

"Don't you think so any longer?"

"Yes, I guess so. If I didn't I'd probably quit tomorrow and serve humanity by digging ditches or something."

"Where did you come from?"

"A little place called Durham. You probably haven't even heard of it."

"Yes I have. I held a series of meetings there a few years ago."

Phinnamore brightened up. "You didn't! Well I'll be! I returned there after seminary and held a pastorate for seven and a half years. In fact, that's where I met my wife and we were married in the church by the district superintendent."

"Did Mrs. Phinnamore come from Durham, too?"

"Not from Durham, but pretty close by. A small hamlet called Gardenvale. Ever hear of it?"

"Yes, there's a lake nearby with good pike fishing, isn't there?"

"That's right. Beth's father owned the local feed mill. Perhaps you heard of him, Nat McLaughlin?"

"No, can't say that I have. All I really remember the place for was the fishing and the large sanitorium up on the hill. Twin Acres, I think it's called."

Phinnamore reacted slightly. "Yes, Twin Acres. It's a beautiful place from the outside, but filled with heartbreak inside."

"Were you ever there?"

"Yes, many times I. . . ." Phinnamore caught himself. "I used to visit some members of my church who were in there, but that was a long time ago."

"I've never had much to do with that type of hospital," said Brainerd. "There are compensations in being an evangelist. You don't have to get involved with the congregation the same way a pastor does."

Phinnamore began to grow visibly uneasy once again. "I'd give anything to never have seen the inside of it. There are too many memories attached."

"Personal memories?"

Phinnamore's eyes flashed. "What do you mean personal? What are you driving at? You want something, what is it?"

Brainerd reached into his coat pocket and removed the envelope Doug Mullen had given him. "I'm going to be honest with you."

"That's refreshing," shot back Phinnamore. "You'll be one of the few around here that is."

"I don't want to upset you unduly, but there is something you should know and now's the time to tell you. I'm working with Inspector Potter on the Scales' murder case."

Brainerd watched Phinnamore closely as he sank deeper into the chair. "Why didn't you tell me this at the beginning?"

"It wouldn't have done any good. I had to try and get you to open up. You see, Potter thinks that there is more to this than just a straight murder. He's sure that somehow, you're involved."

"You mean he suspects me?"

"No, but he thinks that you can answer a lot of questions."

"How can I? He questioned me and I told him everything I know."

"Did you? Who are you protecting?"

"No one. Who is there to protect?"

"Your wife!"

"Beth, what's she got to do with it? She wasn't even near the church. I can prove it."

"No one ever said she was but she's involved just the same. I have no official capacity. I'm just trying to help. Won't you let me?"

"There's nothing to help. I didn't kill Charlie—neither did Beth."

Brainerd sucked in his breath. "All right, I'd hoped you would tell me on your own. Let's go back a bit. You said that you came from Durham and Mrs. Phinnamore from Gardenvale. Right?"

"Yes, what about it?"

"You also said you were married and spent the first seven and a half years of your married life in Durham. Stop me if I'm incorrect."

"Go ahead, you seem to know all the answers."

"Have you and Mrs. Phinnamore any children?"

Phinnamore's face hardened and his mouth became a thin slit. "No, we haven't."

"Did you ever have any?"

"No."

"Well, someone's made a mistake then." Brainerd unfolded a piece of heavy paper. "Here is a photostatic copy of a birth certificate dated June 7, 1927, listing Harrison James Phinnamore and Beth Ann Phinnamore, nee McLaughlin, as the parents of twin girls named Sandra Lee and Joyce Ann. . . ."

"That's enough," breathed Phinnamore as he rose and closed the living room door. "Don't ever mention what you just said in front of my wife."

He returned to his chair and wrung his hands. Suddenly Brainerd was aware that Phinnamore was a very old and tired man.

"Want to tell me about it?"

"I'm sorry—I didn't mean to lie. We have no children, and as far as we are concerned we never had. Can you understand that?"

"I think so, but you'd better explain."

Phinnamore cleared his throat. "Do you have any children?"

"Yes, a boy and a girl. Why?"

"Did your wife have a difficult time at childbirth?"

"No more than any other woman I suppose."

"You're a fortunate man and your wife's fortunate too. Beth nearly died. She was in labor for twenty-three hours and would have slipped away if the doctor hadn't forced the birth. We were happy—they were beautiful girls." His voice started to quiver. "When Beth brought the girls home from the hospital her mother came and stayed with her for the first few weeks. As soon as she got back on her feet she wanted to be on her own, so her mother left. Everything was wonderful, we were so happy. Then it happened."

"What happened?"

"Beth had what the doctor called a post partum psychosis, or in simple terms a nervous breakdown, following the birth of the girls. It's really quite common. It is hard to pinpoint just when or how it started. Beth would forget things, little things. Then she started to turn on the girls. She complained about the washing, the crying and the getting up to feed them at night. You know all the things which every mother has to put up with. I started to get concerned, especially one night when I returned from a prayer meeting and found the girls screaming in their cribs. They were soaking wet and Beth was blissfully asleep on the bed beside them. I told the doctor, but in those days medicine wasn't as advanced. He just said she was tired, gave her some sleeping pills and told me to help more."

Brainerd leaned forward in his chair, "Go on."

"It was all my fault. I should never have left her."

"What was your fault?"

"Everything. If I hadn't gone without Beth perhaps she never would have done it."

"Done what?"

"Killed our little girls, that's what." Phinnamore broke down and began to sob.

"I'm sorry I had to put you through this. Believe me I am, but it had to be done. You see, Inspector Potter is a thorough policeman. When the case got bogged down and it looked like the investigation had reached a dead end Potter moved into high gear and put all his years of training and experience to work. He began by listing on a large blackboard everyone at Fairview who was directly involved with the church or Charlie Scales. Then he laboriously delved into their backgrounds to see if there were any correlating facts which would tie one or more together. Since you and Jimmy were first on the list he stopped when he dug up the unfortunate circumstances surrounding your children. What happened to Mrs. Phinnamore?"

"They found her innocent by reason of insanity and had her committed to Twin Acres. I wanted her somewhere else, but the doctor thought she would come around quicker if she were near her family. Quicker. It took her five years! That's why I spent the first seven and a half years of my marriage in Durham. I had to. Twin Acres has changed a lot since those days. Even the name is different. Then it was called the county asylum."

"A lot of things have changed since those days," said Brainerd.

"Since you know all this perhaps you have figured out how it's tied-in with what's going on at the church?"

"I have an idea, but suppose you tell me your side of it."

"I'm being blackmailed!"

"We thought as much once we learned about Mrs. Phinnamore. Who is it?"

"Can you believe it? I don't know. I've been paying this leech every cent I can scrape up for the past two years and I don't know who he is. Isn't that a laugh?"

"If you don't know who it is how do you pay him?"

"Each month I either receive a typed letter in the mail or a telephone call instructing me how to make the payment and how much."

"Why pay him? How much does he know?"

"Everything, he knows everything. He sent me a photostatic copy of Beth's admission form when she was committed along with copies of the babies' birth certificates. He said that if I ever missed a payment he would send the local paper a story about the murder and pinpoint Beth."

"No editor in his right mind would use a thing like that. Why didn't you call his bluff?"

"I tried to once. He said that if I didn't get back in line he would send a duplicate copy to every member at Fairview. That would either kill Beth or put her right back into an institution. Either way I'd lose her and I couldn't take the chance."

"Aren't you going to fight back?"

"With what? I considered everything, including murder. One month he had me mail the money to a Mr. Smith, care of general delivery at the main post office in the city. I thought this time I would get him for sure. I went and hung around the post office for two and a half days, but he never showed. Do you know what I was going to do?"

"No?"

"I had a revolver in my pocket. I was going to kill him. Me, a minister of the Gospel, contemplating the death of one of God's children and then getting up in the pulpit the next Sunday and preaching a message on forgiveness. Little wonder my ministry was suffering and people were beginning to talk, eh?"

"You were under a pretty heavy strain. Tell me something?"

"What else do you want to know?"

"Were you at the church with Jimmy on the night Scales was murdered?"

Phinnamore rubbed his hands together. "What's the use? I might as. well tell you. Yes, I was there with Jimmy. I was purposely a day late in paying the money. He phoned me and made all kinds of threats. I had an idea that if I could aggravate him enough he might be forced to reveal who he was. It was driving me crazy not knowing. I started taping every telephone call he made, then when he called that night I told him I was turning the tapes over to the police and would let them handle it."

"You weren't serious were you?"

"No, but he didn't know it. I played one of the tapes over to him just to show him that I wasn't kidding. He went wild. Demanded that I send all the tapes to him along with the money or he would do physical harm to me and Beth. I told him that they were well hidden and let it slip that they weren't in the house. He put two and two together as I thought he would and figured that I must have them in my study at the church. I had to do something with Beth so planned to leave her with Betty. I telephoned Jimmy and asked him to meet me at the church in an hour. I said I wanted to go over some program agendas. It must have taken me nearly an hour to get Beth moving and dropped off at the Ferguson's. I had it all planned out that I would send Jimmy on a wild goose chase after some Sunday school material and hide in the church. There was a spot in the choir-loft where I could hide and see my office through the door which the choir entered. When I got there the study was a shambles. I never thought he would get there so fast. Frankly, I think he was hiding in the church when I got there, but I can't be sure."

"What happened when Jimmy arrived? What did you tell him?"

"I took him in and showed him the study. I was pretty evasive, but let on that something was wrong and I was involved. I implied that for his own sake I couldn't admit that I was even with him that night and would have to lie about it if necessary. Just as we were leaving after cleaning up the place I got a call from the maniac."

"Did Jimmy hear your conversation?"

"No, I told him to go out and wait for me in his car. I guess that's when Harry Boland happened to drive by. That was an unfortunate bit of timing. Of all the people, Harry Boland."

"What time was that?"

"Oh, about ten-thirty."

"What did he say on the phone?"

"I don't really remember. I know he babbled on as he usually did and then I got mad. I told him that if he ever pulled a stunt like that again I wouldn't be responsible for what I would do."

"What did he say to that?"

"He told me to shut up and do what I was told."

"What did you do?"

"I shut up and did what I was told."

"Why do you suppose Jimmy didn't tell Potter about being with you?"

"Because I asked him not to, that's why."

"He could have been convicted you know. Many have been on a lot shakier evidence."

"I wouldn't have let that happen. You believe me, don't you?"

"Yes, I believe you. Are you willing to tell Potter what you've just told me?"

"Does Beth have to know or become involved?"

"It's not up to me, but I can't see why she couldn't be kept out of it."

"All right, let's get it over with. Perhaps there's a chance that the whole mess can be cleared up once and for all, eh?"

"I think the chances are better than they've ever been. May I use your phone?"

Phinnamore opened the living room door and led Brainerd out into the hall to where the phone was.

"Please be discreet. I don't want Beth to catch on," he whispered.

"Don't worry, she'll never hear it from me."

Brainerd dialed and turned his back to Phinnamore. "Inspector, Paul. Reverend Phinnamore and I would like to see you as soon as possible. Yes, things are beginning to fit into place. We'll be right down."

Phinnamore had returned to the living room and was standing by the window. "What did he say?"

"He'll see us as soon as we can get to his office. Can you leave right away?"

"Certainly, I'll just tell Beth not to wait up for me." Phinnamore disappeared upstairs.

As they reached the front door Phinnamore took Brainerd by the arm. "Will you tell me something?"

"If I can."

"What else was in that envelope besides Beth's admission record?"

"Photostats of the police reports covering the death of your children."

Phinnamore thought for a moment. "What would you have done if I'd refused to tell you everything?"

"I'd have shown them to your wife."

Chapter 13

POTTER WALKED BACK and forth in front of the office window, occasionally stopping long enough to relight his pipe and squint out at the street below through the venetian blinds. Seated at the side of his desk was a police stenographer who seldom looked up from her book as Phinnamore talked. Brainerd was slumped down in an uncomfortable wingback chair, his collar open and tie pulled down. He looked like anything but one of the country's outstanding evangelists.

"That's about it, Inspector," said Phinnamore with obvious relief registering in his voice.

"Did you get it?" Potter directed his question at the stenographer.

"Yes, sir. It's all down."

"Good, will you please get on it right away? I want a transcript as quickly as possible."

"Will tomorrow morning do, sir?"

"No, tomorrow morning will not do. I want it tonight; in fact I want it within the hour. Do I make myself clear?"

"Yes, sir, quite. I'll start right now." The girl scurried out of the room, nearly tripping over Brainerd's outstretched feet which he made no attempt to move.

"Well now, Reverend Phinnamore, that's quite a tale you've just told. Do you have the tape and letters with you?"

Brainerd lifted one foot and pointed with his toe to a large brown envelope. "They're all there, Inspector."

Potter rubbed his hands and pushed a button on the intercom.

"Sergeant, will you please bring in a tape-recorder and have Mullen come to my office? What do you mean, he's left the station? Get him back here if you have to send a car after him. This isn't a nine to five office I'm running." He flicked the button up with his index finger.

Brainerd thought he noted traces of a smile on Potter's face but refrained from mentioning it.

The officer came in with the tape-recorder and put on the reel which Potter thrust into his hand as he sat down in the swivel chair behind his cluttered desk. Spinning to face those in the room he said, "Please be as quiet as possible. I want to listen to this tape carefully."

For the next half hour no one spoke or moved unnecessarily. Potter's face was impassive as he strained to catch some of the words which were difficult to hear because of the rasping voice.

The door to the office opened and Doug Mullen slipped into the room. Potter didn't even indicate he noticed him except for a slight frown which crossed his face as the door clicked shut.

A moment later he said, "Stop the tape and go back. I missed some of that when our late friend decided to honor us with his presence."

"Sorry, Inspector, I thought you had wrapped it up for the day. I suppose I should have checked?"

"You should have checked," replied Potter. "Now then we shall try once again. Play that tape back in its entirety, Sergeant. I want you to listen to it carefully, Doug, and tell me if you hear anything which brings back memories."

"What's on the tape?"

Potter let a lungful of air escape through his clenched teeth and raising a hand, said, "Hold it for a moment, Sergeant, while I bring my colleague up-to-date."

Once Potter had outlined in point form what had transpired he indicated with a wave of his hand for the tape to be rerun.

The intensity of his concentration was deeper than before. Occasionally he watched those in the room out of the corner of his eye. For the most part, however, he leaned back in his chair not taking his eyes off the whirring tape.

The officer snapped the recorder off and looked over at Potter. "That's all for now, Sergeant. I'll call if I need you again."

"Thank you, sir," replied the officer as he started to lift the machine off the table.

"Leave it here. We may want to listen to some more. It looks like we're in for a long night."

Potter got up from his desk and swung the portable blackboard around. In orderly rows were the names of the council members of Fairview. All had blank spaces alongside except two and these were solidly filled in.

Phinnamore looked closely at the board and said, "so that's how you do it."

"Do what?" asked Potter.

"Dissect a man bit by bit."

"Yes, I was just getting into the swing of things when we landed on that information about Mrs. Phinnamore. It was one of those happy breaks. You see, the best place to begin is with the police. The first thing I did on you and Ferguson was contact the police where you used to live. I asked them if they had anything of interest on record. It paid off this time."

"What would you have done if they hadn't anything?"

"Kept right on checking until I got something." Potter took a brush and erased the board.

Mullen got up and said, "Here, let me do that."

"Well, thank you," replied Potter. "It was worth bringing you back if only for that."

Mullen ignored the remark and began wiping the board clean.

Potter picked up a piece of chalk and faced those in the room. "Gentlemen, I'm going to put you all to work. Each one of you heard the conversations and each one of you heard them differently. I'll go around the room and I want to know what you thought you heard. I want you to try and give me a mental picture of just what you think the speaker is like. Let's begin with you, Paul."

Potter wrote in point form as each one gave his impressions. When he'd finished with Mullen, whom he'd left to the last, he filled in the blank space with his name on top, then turned around from the blackboard. "Not bad at all. You are a very attentive group.

100

Take a look at each column and you will see some interesting similarities and differences."

The room was quiet as each man studied the four columns.

Mullen was the first to speak. "That looks awful familiar, Inspector, awful familiar."

"Just what I was thinking myself, Doug."

"What looks familiar, Inspector?" asked Brainerd.

"You tell him, Doug."

Mullen rose and walked toward the blackboard taking the pointer which Potter handed across the desk.

"First, look at the answer to the Inspector's question about the voice. You sir," he pointed to Phinnamore, "said that it sounded like someone who suffered from allergies or asthma. Paul said that it could be the result of the person trying to disguise his voice."

Brainerd interrupted. "I did say that I was not definite, if you'll remember. If it was self-induced we're dealing with a very good actor."

"Precisely, Paul, that's what I would have said up to two years ago. Now I'll bet my next week's pay along with the Inspector that the wheezing's faked."

"How can you be so definite?" asked Phinnamore.

Potter stood up and walked over to the blackboard. "Let me have a go, Doug."

Mullen nodded his assent and returned to his chair beside Brainerd.

"About two years ago Doug and I were sent on a course to the police college. One of the newer detection sciences we studied in depth was voice printing."

"Voice printing?" Phinnamore knitted his forehead. "Never heard of it."

"Not many people have, sir. Let me explain." Potter looked over at Mullen. "Got all this down on the board, Doug?"

"Yes, sir."

"Fine." Potter rubbed out the writing. "Each one of us possesses three peculiarly personal characteristics which cannot be completely camouflaged or obliterated—our voice, our fingerprints and our handwriting. We were shown how the voice pattern remains the

101

same no matter how it is disguised. By using a machine equipped with a special paper and a stylus pen tracings were made of someone talking normally. The same person was asked to change his voice in any manner he wanted to. Some raised it, some lowered it, while others faked an accent. No matter how they disguised it, the voice patterns were the same. This technique has already been used and admitted in court as evidence in the United States."

"What's all this going to achieve? We don't know who the person is so how can you compare his real voice with the telephone voice?" asked Phinnamore.

"That's where you come in, Reverend."

"Come in where? Do you think he's the murderer as well?"

"I think the chances are very good that he is. If he isn't, I still want him. Blackmail is one of the dirtiest charges on the books and I want him on that, if nothing else."

"What do you want me to do?"

"Get him mad. In fact get him so steamed that he'll lose control and make a mistake."

"How?"

"By not meeting his demands and turning the tables on him. You're going to indulge in a bit of blackmail yourself." Potter rubbed his hands with satisfied relish.

"How can you blackmail a blackmailer?"

"How did he blackmail you, Reverend?"

"You know very well. He obtained that information about Beth, knew I wouldn't want it made known and put the squeeze on me for money."

Potter was in high spirits. "I'm going to give you some information about our friend and you're going to sell it to him."

"For money?"

"Not on your life. For something far more valuable—his neck."

Phinnamore appeared in a fog, but Brainerd, his eyes darting back and forth, took everything in.

Potter tapped out his pipe and looked over at Brainerd. "Well, Paul, you've been conspicuous by your silence. What do you think?"

102

"I think you're a sly one, Inspector."

Potter stroked his chin, making a rasping sound as his fingers grazed the stubble of his beard. "Do you now?"

Brainerd's eyes narrowed. "I certainly do. Furthermore, I think you've got things clear in your mind and are ready to move. Am I right?"

"Right as rain. Now, then, let's get going." Potter erased the blackboard once again, leaving broad roads of chalk dust which he made no attempts to remove. "I think that we'll all agree we're dealing with an unknown quantity inasmuch as we don't know who the blackmailer really is. On the other hand, if he is the murderer he's keeping a pretty close watch on what we're doing and trying to figure out just how much we really do know. The big advantage is that he doesn't know we're trying to connect his blackmailing efforts to the killing. In fact, I seriously doubt that he suspects we're even considering his shakedown game at this time. This is where we have the advantage and this is where we're going to strike."

"You mean we're forgetting the murder for the time being?" asked Mullen.

"Exactly, we're forgetting all about the murder and going after a blackmailer. If you recall, I mentioned a few moments ago that everyone has three characteristics which they cannot completely hide. We can positively tie in two of these right now with the blackmailer, so by using a little bit of, shall we say, police license, we may get our man without needing the third."

Potter unfolded the blackmail letters which Phinnamore had received and spread them out on the table in order of dates.

"Our man was very careless in a couple of instances, look here."

The other men crowded around Potter.

"These dates are not in a disguised handwriting. He was very careful to obviously alter the body of the letter but, through course of habit, wrote the date in what I'll bet is his normal hand."

Brainerd, picking up two, held them up to the light. "He's right. The April in this letter and the September in this one are similar. Inspector, I'll bet a graphologist could come up with something."

103

"So do I, Paul, and I intend to find out."

Phinnamore returned to his chair and said, "I don't mean to sound foolish, but isn't graphology something you see demonstrated in a side-show at a fall fair?"

"Not as far as the police are concerned," answered Mullen. "I've read about many cases which used this technique to either prove or disprove the legality of a document. It's a proven fact that a skilled graphologist can analyze a specimen of someone's writing and tell you pretty factually just what that person is like. They can tell you even if they are emotionally unstable because someone suffering from an incipient disease will betray it by a slight tremor in his writing."

Potter picked up a piece of chalk and walked to the blackboard. "Let's recap what we already know. If I miss anything, speak up."

He began writing under two headings, proven and unproven. When he had finished he turned around and placed his hands on his hips.

"This may appear academic, but I have a reason for it. Paul said I had a plan and he's right. Each one of you here are part of that plan and if it's going to have a ghost of a chance of succeeding you'll have to know as much about this case as I do. Let's examine what we have. Under proven I've listed the main points we know for sure about the blackmailer. We know that he's a creature of habit. This is obvious from the organized times he contacts Mr. Phinnamore every month with his instructions. It's always around the twenty-sixth or seventh. Has he ever changed that pattern, Mr. Phinnamore?"

Phinnamore thought for a moment. "No. I can think of only once when Beth and I were out of town. He was quite upset because he couldn't reach me. He ordered me not to take off like that again unless I told him the month before."

"That's the point I'm trying to make. The strongest thing we have going for us is his dislike of anything which upsets his plans. We know that he can also be moved to physical action if the stimulation is great enough. This is proven by the office episode. Since we know this much we can now move over to the unknown side of the ledger. We don't know how old he is, what he looks like, or where he came from. In fact we know relatively little about him except that he is an organized individual who hates to have his plans upset and will react violently."

"You said that the murder was not a consideration at this point, Inspector, why not?"

"Well, Doug, have you ever considered the fact that we might be really after two men instead of one? There's a strong possibility that the blackmailer and murderer are not one and the same. What would you say to the theory that the blackmailer only intended to throw a scare into Mr. Phinnamore and was just as surprised as anybody that there was a murder in the church?"

"I'd say that it was a good theory, but not too likely. Personally, I think the evidence points to just one man."

"I'm inclined to agree with you, but I'm keeping an open mind for the time being." Potter stood in front of Phinnamore. "Are you up to being the catalyst which brings the blackmailer and me together?"

Phinnamore stiffened. "Yes, by all means. I only wish that I'd told you all about it right from the start. What do you want me to do?"

"Nothing, absolutely nothing!"

"Nothing? I thought you just asked me to help?"

"I did, and by doing nothing you'll be leaving yourself wide open to a very dangerous situation. Today is the twenty-second of July. According to the pattern established you'll be contacted in four or five days with instructions of where to leave or send the money. I want you to act as though nothing has happened to change things and say or do nothing that would scare him off. Once he's contacted you the plan begins. I'm sending the tape and letters to our laboratory for immediate analysis. I should have the report back in two days at the most. It won't tell me much more than I know already, but it will permit you to honestly tell whoever it is that you know a good deal about him and are going to the police with the information. Try and make a deal, if he'll give you all his blackmail evidence you'll give him yours. That should be enough to really set him off."

"Why would he believe that I had anything?"

"Because you will have. The police department will supply it for you."

"I can't tell him that I went to the police. He's told me many times not to try it unless I was willing to face the consequences."

Potter opened his desk drawer and took out a folded newspaper. "Any of you read last night's paper?"

Each one shook his head.

"Tomorrow night is the official open house of our new headquarters building and the public is invited to come and see how their police department works. There'll be demonstrations all over the building in which the visitors will be invited to take part. Two of the demonstrations will cover voice printing and graphology. In order to make it more interesting the public has been invited to bring in samples of handwriting and tapes of voices for analysis. The advertising suggests that they can be as wild as possible so that the experts will really be put to the test. They'll leave them and receive a written report in a few days."

"Isn't it a bit far-fetched to think that someone as devious as the blackmailer will fall for something like this? It's almost theatrical," asked Phinnamore.

"I don't think so," replied Potter. "I'm going on the assumption that he's not a professional and that's why he reacts so violently to any change in his plans. In fact, I'll bet this is his first time at it and he's scared stiff."

"If that's the case why doesn't he stop?"

"A good question, Reverend. I'm not a psychologist, but I've seen enough to make me convinced that he probably can't stop and deep down really hopes that he'll be caught. Agree, Paul?"

"Sounds reasonable, Inspector. I think that whoever it is, is desperate, especially if he's the murderer. He'll probably be willing to kill again. After all you know the old saying, 'the first one's the hardest, the next one comes easier,' or something like that."

"Well I think we're all agreed that this is our chance to move and see if we can push our friend hard enough to do something foolish. I want you to be quite obvious tomorrow night at the open house. I'll arrange with the police photographer to have a picture

106

taken of you talking with our graphologist and have it run in the morning paper. The cutline will say something about 'Local minister finds science of voice printing and handwriting analysis fascinating at police department open house'."

"Won't that look a bit obvious?" asked Phinnamore.

"We have to be obvious. There isn't time to be subtle. Once that appears and you stall him on the payment we'll have the two weapons we need to prod him. Now then, I want what you say to him to be letter perfect and plausible. I'll not have you compromise your calling by telling lies. Whatever material I give you will have gone through the various analysis. In this way I think that you can be much more believable."

"That's a good idea. I always was a poor liar."

"What do you want Paul and me to do, Inspector?"

"Be ready to move quickly when I need you. I want you, Doug, to stay with Mr. and Mrs. Phinnamore practically night and day once this begins. You have some holidays coming up so I want you to take them and start painting the parsonage as your contribution to the work at Fairview. Can you announce from the pulpit your appreciation of the offer?"

"Sure, as a matter of fact the men of the church usually give a day or so each year to fix up the house so it will be completely natural. I'll emphasize how appreciative we are of a new member helping out in this manner."

"What a way to spend a holiday!"

"Don't worry—it'll only be a holiday as far as everyone else is concerned. You'll get your full vacation."

Mullen smiled at Phinnamore. "I'm not a very good painter."

Potter spoke before Phinnamore could reply. "Paul, I want you to be ready to take over as soon as the contact has been made. I can't show myself around the church because I'd be recognized immediately. We can't afford to scare him off. I'll be pulling the strings from behind and in constant touch. Whenever Doug finishes his day's work and has to leave you'll take over by visiting the Phinnamore's. In this way we can give practically twenty-four hour coverage. I don't think he'll try anything during the night. In any case, I'll have the house staked out from the outside. Any questions?"

"Just one, Inspector."

"Yes, Mr. Phinnamore?"

"What happens if it doesn't work and someone else gets killed?"

Potter's teeth clicked shut on the stem of his pipe as he drew in a lungful of smoke. He leaned back in his chair and blew the purple cloud up at the ceiling. "Well, Reverend, I'll probably be out of a job and you'll be busy conducting a funeral. Anything else?"

"Nothing, Inspector, I understand perfectly."

Chapter 14

THE SUMMER SUN SLIPPED below the horizon like a fiery meteorite which had found its final resting place. Red and blue fingers streaked the sky as the blazing heat of the day gave way to the refreshing shadows of evening.

Ferguson wiped a forehand across his eyes and squinted at the stop light, trying to see if the red had changed to green. The glare from the sky was still strong enough to make driving an effort, especially when you were facing into it. A blast from the horn of the car behind indicated that the light had changed so he jammed his foot on the accelerator and the car leaped forward.

He was not looking forward to the meeting and wished that he had been able to think of an excuse to get out of it. Betty's uneasiness hadn't helped either. She didn't want him to go unless he told either Brainerd or Potter first. Potter was out of the office when he called and he didn't know where Brainerd was.

As he pulled into the crowded parking lot he thought he recognized the leaf green convertible parked at the end of the row, but he wasn't positive.

Pushing open the door of the restaurant he was greeted by a blast of cool air and stopped for a moment as it bathed his head and shoulders.

"Jim, over here," came a voice from the rear booth.

Ferguson turned and walked between the row of tables.

"Hello, Steve, it's been a long time."

Steve Gordon stood up and held out his hand. "Too long, Jim.

That's why I asked you to meet me. I thought it was high time we forgot the past and took up where we left off."

Ferguson was puzzled. "Why here?"

"No reason, I figured it might be easier if we met by ourselves. After all, two men can usually talk things out if there are no women around."

Ferguson was evasive and aloof. "What's there to talk over?"

"That's just the point, Jim, we should talk things over." Just then a waitress came for their order.

"You don't have to feel apologetic, Steve, I understand."

"No, you don't, I was a fool and I'm sorry. I realize I was wrong in acting the way I did. I hope you can understand, Charlie and I were friends for a long time. It really shook me when he was murdered."

"Let's forget it, eh? I've had all I want of Charlie Scales and his murder." Ferguson's voice was abrasive.

Gordon swallowed a mouthful of iced tea. "All right, let's forget it. Friends?"

"Sure, friends," replied Ferguson without too much enthusiasm.

"What are you and Betty doing for the weekend?"

"I don't know. Why?"

"How about coming up to the cottage with Muriel and me? We could leave Friday night and come back early Sunday morning in time for church."

"I'll have to ask Betty."

"Good, Muriel will be pleased. I hope you can arrange it."

Both men finished their tea and passed the time talking about incidentals. If there was one thing Ferguson hated it was small talk, but there seemed nothing else for the occasion. The friendship was rekindled, but the strain was still evident.

As they got up to leave, Gordon said, "Can you give me a lift?"

"Sure, but wasn't that your car parked at the rear of the lot?"

"No, I was dropped off by a fellow at the office. Muriel has the car today for shopping."

Ferguson made a point to see if the convertible was still there, but it was gone.

"Where do you want me to drop you off, at home?"

"No, could you go by way of Bleeker Street? I want to see a fellow. He's got a boat for sale. I'm thinking of getting it for the lake."

"I thought you had a boat?"

"Sure, but I want a larger one and this looks like a good buy."

"Boy! It must be nice to be loaded."

"Don't kid yourself. Muriel doesn't even know I'm looking. She'd have a fit. I'd appreciate it if you wouldn't mention it to her."

"Makes no difference to me. Now where did you say this place was?"

"Bleeker Street, just drop me off at the corner of Bleeker and Empress, I'll walk."

"Don't you want me to wait?"

"No thanks, I don't want to hold you up. I'll get this guy to drive me home. After all, if I decide to buy his boat it should be worth a ride home."

Ferguson shrugged his shoulders indifferently and turned on the car radio. It seemed like miles, but in fact it was only a few blocks until Gordon touched his arm.

"You can pull in here, Jim, I can walk the rest of the way. It's just around the corner."

"O.K, but I'd be glad to wait for you," replied Ferguson as he pulled up and stopped.

"Thanks just the same, I appreciate it. Be sure to ask Betty about the weekend. I'll give you a call tomorrow." Gordon was out of the car and with a wave of his hand walked off down the street.

Ferguson was curious. He waited for Gordon to turn the corner before taking his foot off the brake and letting the car slowly ease down the street. As he came to the corner, he could see Gordon's form disappear into the darkness of a large veranda. The street had a slight downgrade and the car gently coasted past the house into which Gordon had disappeared. It was a typical house for the neighborhood. Once, no doubt, it had been the mark of gracious living. Now, it could be best described as an income residence—in other words, a rooming house.

Ferguson hoped that the gathering dusk would keep him from being too obvious or recognized. In the front window was a sign illuminated by a bare veranda light which read, "Rooms by Day or Week. Apply Within."

Doug Mullen struggled to balance the ladder as he swung it under the eavestrough.

"Here, let me give you a hand," said Phinnamore as he reached up and hung tightly onto a rung.

"Thanks, I thought for a moment that I was going to send it through the bedroom window," replied Mullen.

By manipulating the ladder and balancing it with his foot on the lower rung Mullen finally got it into place.

"I told the Inspector that I was a lousy painter, but he wouldn't believe me. Not only am I a lousy painter, I hate ladders and all they stand for."

Phinnamore laughed. "Better do a good job or I'll have.to report you to the chief the next time I see him."

"How about seeing him right now? Maybe I'd get taken off this assignment."

Mrs. Phinnamore came to the side of the veranda and called, "Harrison, the telephone, it's for you."

"Thanks, I'll be right in."

"Don't forget, if it's him stall for a moment and call me. I'll only take a second to switch on the tape recorder," instructed Mullen.

As he waited for Phinnamore to return or call, Mullen looked at his watch. It was two-thirty in the afternoon. The call or letter should be coming anytime if the pattern was followed.

Phinnamore came out the back door and around the house to where Mullen was standing at the bottom of the ladder.

"It wasn't him, just one of the members asking about some church business."

"You know something that's bothered me?" asked Mullen.
"What?"

"How come your wife isn't suspicious after all these months?"
"Suspicious about what?"

"The telephone calls and the letters. Doesn't she ever ask what's going on?"

"No, she leaves all the business up to me and never asks."

112

"What happens when he calls and she answers?"

"He either hangs up or says it's a wrong number. She often tells me how annoying it is to come up from the cellar only to have the party hang up just as she says hello or it's a wrong number. I once told him if he ever involved Beth I'd go right to the police."

"Would you've?"

"I doubt it, but I had to tell him something."

Mullen picked up the paint and brush and looking up the ladder said, "Well, here goes, I may never come down."

Paul Brainerd let the car roll to a stop under the shade of a large maple tree whose branches stretched out over the street. He looked at his watch and switched on the car radio.

As he drummed his fingers on the steering wheel, keeping time to the music, he was miles away in thought. The events of the last couple of days were racing around in his mind as he attempted to put them into perspective.

Suddenly the car door sprung open and Inspector Potter slid into the seat.

"You look surprised."

Brainerd shook his head as if to clear the cobwebs. "No, I was just deep in thought, trying to get everything clear in my mind."

"Sorry I had to meet you like this, but I don't want to take the chance of being seen around the church or at Phinnamore's house."

"That's all right, what's up?"

"I think tonight should do it, look here."

Potter unfolded a newspaper. The lead story on the front page, second section, was about the open house at the police headquarters. Right in the middle of the page was a picture of Phinnamore and the police graphologist with a suitable description underneath.

"Just like the movies, eh?"

"Great, how did you swing that?"

"I've friends, believe it or not. It's a good picture and ties in with the story. It should also give our friend about a million fits if his mind works the way I think it does."

"What do you want me to do?"

"Be at the Phinnamore house sharp at five. I've got to get Doug out of there by then or it will look suspicious. I've had Doug arrange with Mr. Phinnamore for you to stay the night."

"How did you manage that?"

"Mr. Phinnamore will want to go over your crusade plans and it will take you well into the early morning. He's going to suggest that you just stay the night in the guest room. It will save disturbing the Fergusons at such a late hour."

"You don't miss a trick, do you?"

"No, I hope not. Now if you get contacted I want our original plan followed. Phinnamore is to act as if everything is all right and say nothing to give it away. If, however, our friend reacts unexpectedly I want you to take charge. I've got the place covered from the outside. If you can't call, flick on the veranda light, leave it on for two minutes, then turn it off. I'll get to you somehow."

"Do you expect him to try and reach Phinnamore personally?"

"You never can tell. I don't intend to take a chance."

"All right, I'll be there just before Doug leaves."

"Good, one thing more. What's Ferguson been up to?"

"Why?"

"I've had him tailed for the past week and last night he met Steve Gordon in a restaurant. Did he tell you about it?"

"Yes, why the tail?"

"I think he might be marked and I don't want him getting hurt. What did he say?"

"He seems genuinely confused by the whole thing. He said Gordon telephoned him and asked him to meet at the restaurant."

"I thought they weren't friends any longer."

"So did Jimmy. Evidently Gordon had an attack of conscience and wanted Jimmy to forget what had happened and start all over again. In fact, he's invited Jimmy and Betty up to their cottage for the weekend."

"Are they going?"

"He's not sure. What do you think?"

"I don't know. Tell him not to accept until he sees me."

"Well," said Brainerd as he started the motor. "I'd better get moving if I'm to be on time. Can I drop you anywhere, Inspector?"

114

Potter opened the door and stepped out. "No thanks, Paul. Take it easy tonight, we've got a live one on our hands."

Paul Brainerd opened the cellar door and called, "Betty, Jim, anybody home?"

"Just a second, Paul, I'll be right up," replied Betty.

Brainerd met her half way down the cellar steps and took the laundry basket out of her hands. "Here, let me, that's too big a load for a petite young girl."

"Well, thank you, kind sir. If you feel that strongly about it you can put in a good word for us with the church council and perhaps they'll see the light."

"What light?"

"The one that will shine night and day over my electric dryer if they put one in."

Brainerd thumped the basket on the kitchen table. "I'll see what can be done. Where's Jimmy?"

"I don't know, I thought he might be with you."

"I haven't seen him since breakfast. Has he given Steve Gordon an answer about the weekend yet?"

"Not unless he talked to him since he left."

"I hope he hasn't. Tell him not to make anything definite until he's talked to Potter."

"What's Potter want?"

"I don't know. That's what he told me to tell Jimmy."

Betty took the laundry out to the back veranda and began hanging it on the line. Brainerd followed her.

"Don't worry about supper for me tonight, I'll be eating at the Phinnamore's."

"Well, if you'd rather eat with the older crowd it doesn't matter to me," mocked Betty.

Brainerd pretended to look hurt. "I'll call and cancel immediately. You and Jimmy will probably be relieved to have dinner by yourself for a change."

"I'll probably have dinner by myself all right if he doesn't hurry up."

"Didn't he say where he was going?"

115

"No, all I know is that he went out after talking to someone on the telephone and said he'd see me later."

"Who was it?"

"I don't know. Someone from the church, I suppose."

Brainerd lowered his head in thought. "If you haven't heard from him by eight give me a call at Phinnamore's."

A worried tone came into Betty's voice. "You don't think anything's wrong, do you?"

Chapter 15

DINNER AT THE Phinnamore's was, as to be expected, a rare treat. Brainerd marveled at the culinary artistry of his hostess and throughout the meal complimented her on the various courses.

"Harrison, why don't you two take your coffee in the living room where you can be more comfortable?"

"Good idea. What do you say, Paul?"

"Fine with me," answered Brainerd as he followed the older man into the room and comfortably situated himself in one of the over-stuffed easy chairs.

Phinnamore waited until his wife began clearing off the dinner table and couldn't hear him. "You don't suppose he's been scared off, do you? I can't ever remember him being so late before."

"No, he'll come through. He has to. They're like the bank robber who says 'just one more, then I'll quit.' He's too much of an egotist to let you off the hook without so much as a good-by."

"I never thought of him as being an egotist."

"Certainly he is. I'll bet he gets as much satisfaction from having you in his power as he does from spending the money."

Phinnamore found the analysis of the blackmailer fascinating and pressed Brainerd for his impressions of the man he had come to know so well, but had never seen. Mrs. Phinnamore sensed that their discussion was private so finished up her work in the kitchen and quietly prepared to retire to her bedroom. She was just about to go upstairs when the harsh ring of the telephone broke through the solitude of the house. Before she could reach the hall table to

117

answer it her husband burst through the French doors leading to the living room.

"I'll get it, Beth, you go ahead upstairs."

"You look guilty, Harrison. You're not expecting a woman to call, are you?"

Phinnamore cut the air with his hand in mock rebuke and picked up the receiver. "Hello, yes, he's right here."

Brainerd was standing in the doorway and took the receiver as it was passed to him. "Yes," he answered and listened carefully.

"Stay right where you are, I'll call back in a few moments. Don't worry we'll find him."

"What is it, Paul?" asked Phinnamore.

"It's Jimmy, he hasn't come home all day. I don't like it." Brainerd dialed the phone and waited, drumming his fingers on the table impatiently.

"Inspector, Paul. No, we haven't heard yet. Something else has come up. Jimmy's missing. No, Betty just phoned and he hasn't come home or tried to call all day. Do you still have a tail on him?"

Brainerd listened intently without saying a word. Finally when Potter had finished issuing instructions he said, "Yes, I've got it clear. I'll be back as soon as we hear about the other."

Phinnamore started to say something but stopped when he saw Brainerd push the disconnect button and twirl the dial without taking the receiver away from his ear.

"Betty, I want you to come over here right away. Don't worry about Jimmy, he'll be all right. Potter's sending a taxi for you in a few moments. Act natural and when you get here, pay the driver and walk calmly up to the front door. Don't run. Have you any money? Good, get ready, the cab will be along in a few moments."

When he replaced the receiver Phinnamore said, "What's happening, what did Potter say?"

Brainerd walked into the living room and sat on the edge of the piano bench. "He wants Betty to stay here until Jimmy's found."

"What was that about a tail on Jimmy?"

"Both of you have been tailed for some time now. Unfortunately, Jimmy lost his."

"On purpose?"

"No, Potter's mad as a wet hen though. Jimmy parked the car in a downtown lot and went into a department store. It was crowded and he slipped into an elevator at the last moment."

"Why didn't the tail go back to his car and pick him up there?"

"He did but Jimmy never came back. His car's still in the lot."

"Are you going to tell Betty?"

"No, and I don't want you to either."

"O.K. I'd better tell Beth to get the spare room ready, looks like you're on the chesterfield."

Brainerd grabbed Phinnamore's arm. "Don't say anything yet. Wait for a while and see what happens. There's no sense getting your wife all upset. She must know something's going on."

Phinnamore nodded his head. "She does. I had to tell her you were helping the police."

"Tell her everything?"

"No, she knows nothing about the blackmail."

"Good."

By the time Betty arrived it was dark. As soon as the cab pulled up the two men were at the front door. Betty played her part well, even to the point of ringing the bell, which was certainly unnecessary. Once inside she began to shake and Brainerd put his arm around her.

"Oh, Paul, I'm so frightened, where's Jimmy?"

"Don't worry, Betty, he'll be all right. Inspector Potter's looking after it, he's the best."

"Jimmy's in trouble, I know he is. It's that horrible man on the telephone, isn't it?"

"Did you get a call?"

"I don't know. The telephone rang just as the cab came, but I was too scared to answer it." Betty put her hand up to her mouth. "What if it was Jimmy and he needed me, oh Paul?"

"If it was Jimmy he'd try here if you weren't home. I'm sure it wasn't him."

Mrs. Phinnamore came into the living room. "I thought I heard Betty's voice. Hello, my dear."

Before Brainerd could stop her Betty ran to the older woman

119

and buried her head on her shoulder. "Jimmy's gone," she sobbed. "He's in trouble, what'll I do?"

"What's going on around here, Harrison?" demanded Mrs. Phinnamore.

Brainerd interrupted. "Could you take Betty upstairs? I'll tell you both all I can in a few moments."

"Come along, my dear, I'll make a cup of tea. It'll be all right, I just know it will."

Brainerd watched as the two women left. "You've quite a woman there."

"I know it, sometimes I think I've underestimated her strength."

Mrs. Phinnamore came into the room carrying a tray with tea and cakes on it. "If you two are going to carry on all night you'll need something in your stomachs."

"You're a real gem, Mrs. Phinnamore. If he doesn't look after you give me a call."

"Mrs. Phinnamore patted her husband's cheek and replied. "That's one thing I've never had to worry about. If you want Betty and me, we'll be in my room. Try not to be too late, Harrison."

"I'll be along just as soon as I can, Beth."

Brainerd waited until she had left the room and was upstairs with Betty. "Is there enough cord so we can bring the phone into the living room?"

Phinnamore nodded and returned with the phone in one hand as he played out the cord with the other. He had just set it down on the coffee table when it began ringing.

Brainerd jumped to his feet. "Hold it until I get the tape recorder," he ordered.

He moved quickly and by the time it had finished the fourth ring indicated to Phinnamore that everything was ready.

Phinnamore lifted the receiver gently. "Hello." He nodded his head vigorously.

Brainerd hovered over the tape recorder making sure that there were no malfunctions.

Phinnamore suddenly straightened up to his full height. "Now you listen to me. I'm sick and tired playing your tune, it's my turn now. I've got positive proof as to your identity. Certainly I made

120

use of the police facilities, you don't think I was going to let a chance like that pass, do you?" He winked at Brainerd.

Phinnamore held the receiver away from his ear so Brainerd could listen. There was silence on the other end except for the labored breathing that had become so familiar.

"You can cut out that phony breathing. I know now it's all an act. That's right, all an act. Do you want me to read the police report on the tapes I let them have? All right let's settle this once and for all. I'm through being bled white by you. I'll make a deal. You give me all your information on my wife and I'll give you what I have on you, tapes, reports, everything—then we're finished. Of course I won't go to the police. What would be the use after all this time? I still want to protect my wife."

Brainerd wrote on a pad in large letters. KEEP HIM GOING, IT'S WORKING!

Phinnamore took a big gulp of air. "You still there? All right here's my offer. I'll exchange what I have for what you've got. Agreed? No, the church is empty, why there?"

Brainerd mouthed the words. "That's all right, tell him you'll meet him there any time he says."

"That's a switch, you asking me," sneered Phinnamore. "O.K, two-thirty in the morning. No, I'll be alone. Yes, I'll leave it open."

Phinnamore stood rooted to the floor as Brainerd switched off the recorder and taking the receiver out of his hand said, "Let me hang this up."

Brainerd immediately rewound the tape and dialed the phone.

"Inspector, he called! Listen to this."

Potter flicked a button and put the phone on conference. "Just a moment, Paul, I want Doug to hear this, it'll save time."

Potter stuck his head out the door of his office and called, "Doug, come here quick."

"What's up?" asked Mullen as he rushed into the office.

Potter held up his hand. "You all ready, Paul?"

"Yes, Inspector, here goes."

121

Both men stared at the conference speaker as the tape was played. When they heard it click off Potter asked, "Is Reverend Phinnamore with you?"

"Yes."

"Put him on."

"Yes, Inspector."

"Congratulations, sir, you carried it off like a real pro. Now are you up to a bit more?"

"I think so, what do you want?"

"I want you to stay where you are and let Paul have your best suit. Put Paul back on."

Brainerd came on the phone and listened silently as Potter outlined his plan. When he had finished he said, "All clear, Paul?"

"Yes, all clear. Have you found Jimmy?"

"No, but it shouldn't be long. I'm staking my reputation on both these being connected."

"Well, I hope you're right because I'm staking my neck on your reputation."

"What are you worried about, Paul? You can always make a living preaching. If I'm wrong, I'm through. The only thing I can do is be a policeman."

"You don't think a minister will have a better career in Heaven, do you?"

Chapter 16

THE CICADAS AND TREE toads had been silent for a number of hours. All that could be heard in the stillness of the night was the rustling of leaves as they were twisted and turned by the unseen hand of a gentle breeze.

Doug Mullen looked at his watch. It was twenty after two. He quietly shifted his numbed legs, rubbing the calf of the left one which was on pins and needles. Trying to squeeze his bulky frame into the choir loft under normal circumstances would have been an accomplishment, but to ask him to squat down on the floor behind the seat was just too much.

The lights in the church were out. The only illumination which cast eerie shadows about the empty auditorium came from the street light on the corner as it filtered through the stained glass windows.

Mullen gripped a small transmitter in his left hand. The receiving unit, which was about the size of a hearing aid set, was in his shirt pocket. A cord ran to the plug in his left ear. He checked to make sure that the volume was turned down to its lowest point. Their operation was quite familiar—he had used them many times before on other stake-outs.

Through the partly opened choir door he could see the outline of the entrance to Phinnamore's office. He didn't mind the waiting, he was used to it. The thing that grated on his nerves was the awkward position he was forced to assume. *I'll bet Potter's comfortable back there in the choir dressing room,* he thought.

Potter's voice came through the earpiece, snapping him to alertness. "Everything quiet?"

"Yes, Inspector, nothing yet."

"O.K, keep on your toes. He should be along any moment."

Mullen shifted his foot and listened. Outside on the street an occasional car pulled to a stop, then roared off into the night. Every sound was magnified. Even the careful shifting of his feet seemed to echo throughout the vacant auditorium.

Potter had rehearsed the plan over and over again with Mullen as he set it up. Under normal circumstances he probably would have gone for full support and ringed the church with men, but this situation was far from normal. He didn't want to run the risk of scaring off his man, possibly for good. With Mullen in the choir loft covering the front approaches and himself in the choir room covering the rear he felt confident that the net was tight. As a last resort he could always call for assistance on the communication set which was tied-in on the police wavebands.

Mullen stiffened. He was sure he heard something. There it was again, a foreign noise, quiet, but nevertheless distinct. He raised himself high enough so that his eyes were level with the top of the seat.

"Inspector," he whispered into the open transmitter, "he's here."

"O.K, I'll cover the hall."

A dark shadow crossed the front vestibule and melted into the blackness at the rear of the auditorium. Mullen wondered how he got in from that point. The back door had been left open as instructed. There was no time to figure out that problem. He squinted, keeping his eyes riveted on the spot where he thought the figure would reappear. Sure enough, there it was, dark and crouching. It eased up the auditorium, pew by pew, stopping every few feet to listen like some wild beast at a watering hole. Mullen followed the movement, his heart beating until he was sure it would explode right through his chest. As the figure came closer Mullen slipped his hand behind his back and gently lifted his service revolver from its holster.

124

Potter tightly gripped his revolver. He thought he'd heard something, too, but it was difficult to be sure. The possibility of making a mistake and concentrating on just one suspect crossed his mind. He made sure that the element of surprise would be on their side. Before taking up his position he'd strung black thread from the legs of a number of chairs in the Sunday school auditorium. It would be impossible for anyone to come up from behind without giving themselves away. There was always the chance that the suspect would somehow come in from that direction, but it was a chance Potter had to take. He purposely left the direct access from the back door to Phinnamore's office unobstructed. All he wanted was to protect himself from being taken unawares by an accomplice.

He eased himself through the door and out into the hall leading to Phinnamore's office. The advantage of being completely surrounded by darkness was his. He watched, nerves taut. This was what he'd been working toward, from the day he received the call to investigate an accident at Fairview Community Church.

The inside of Phinnamore's office was even darker than the church auditorium. The drapes, pulled securely over the window, shut out any light that could possibly seep in. The figure in the chair behind the desk leaned forward, pressing his hands into the desk-top blotter. A cord ran from a plug in his ear to his breast pocket. He could hear Potter and Mullen but was unable to communicate because he didn't have the transmitting unit. Dark as it was, his eyes had gradually adjusted. He could pick out various objects in the room such as the filing cabinet, two chairs, table and door.

The first thing which came into focus was the door, then he concentrated on the knob because that would be the symbol of success. If it turned they would have their man.

A slight brushing outside the door betrayed the presence of someone. It seemed like an eternity until he saw the knob slowly turn and heard it click. The door moved, just a crack at first, then little by little, until it opened wide enough to reveal a hunched figure. Nothing moved. Suddenly, a shaft of light from the desk lamp cut through the blackness!

The intruder let out a startled gasp, shielding his eyes with an arm. Without saying a word he wheeled and raced down the hall toward the church auditorium.

"After him, Doug!" yelled Potter as he ran past the door. "Stay where you are, Paul," he ordered.

By the time Potter reached the front of the church everything had become silent once more. He eased into the auditorium, crouching, gun in hand, trying to adjust his vision. Slowly he rounded the front of the platform keeping as low as possible. He stopped and listened, all was silent. Just as he came level with the pulpit an arm with an object extending from it sliced through the air. Potter crumpled to the floor without saying a word.

Ferguson wished he'd never answered the telephone. If he'd just let it ring he'd probably be at home now with Betty instead of wondering where she was.

He looked at his watch. It was nearly two. How much longer was he going to have to wait? Promise or no promise he was leaving at two-thirty, he'd made up his mind.

The only pleasant aspect about the entire affair was the Chinese food.

Too bad Betty couldn't have been with me, he wished. *Chinese food is for company, not individuals.*

He didn't realize how hungry he was until he smelled the food. It had been nearly twelve hours since he'd eaten. He was relieved that the order had been paid for when it arrived. There were only two one dollar bills in his wallet and no change, not even a quarter to tip the delivery boy.

Ferguson walked over to the window and looked out. There wasn't a soul on the street. Come to think of it the only other people he'd seen since he arrived at the house was the delivery boy and that old lady in the hall early that afternoon.

"Boy," he said to himself, "did she ever give me the once over." He chuckled when he remembered the face he'd made in response

126

to her critical stare. She probably thought he was drunk or in the wrong house.

Suddenly he felt very tired and wanted to go to sleep. He stumbled over to the chesterfield and sprawled out with his feet dangling over the edge.

Off in the mist of his dream world he was conscious of someone coming in the room, putting something between his fingers and moving his hand.

Who is it? What is he trying to do? Didn't he know I want to sleep?

Vaguely Ferguson sensed that he was being eased back onto the chesterfield. Through squinting eyes he thought that he could make out someone clicking the lock and slipping the night chain into place. He couldn't be sure, it was all jumbled like an unrelated dream. The last thing to penetrate his receding consciousness was a shadow near the window.

He must be raising the window, he thought. *I can feel a breeze.*

Everything went silent!

Mullen caught the fleeting silhouette of a figure at the front of the auditorium and raced down the side aisle. As he reached the four steps leading up to the platform he stopped and turned. In front of the pulpit lay a dark form.

Suddenly someone leaped out of the darkness sending him spiralling across the floor toward the front pews. His gun flew up in the air and landed underneath the grand piano. Mullen braced himself for the impact and with professional ease, rolled and leaped to his feet, ready for battle.

The air was rent by thudding bodies and groans. The grand piano chimed like a carillon gone wild as it reeled under the impact of solid flesh. The pace was beginning to tell on both combatants as they crunched to the floor.

Mullen's jaw snapped up as two vice-like hands clenched his throat. A searing blackness was quickly engulfing him . . . he was being strangled!

With the remaining reserve of strength in his body he braced himself and brought both hands up in a slashing double judo chop. They found their mark and caught his attacker across the throat and face. The body went limp and draped itself over Mullen's aching frame.

He stumbled to his feet and grabbing the prone figure on the floor flopped him over on his face. With two metallic clicks the handcuffs were snapped into place.

Brainerd came running through the door. "Doug, Inspector, are you all right?"

"Here, Paul, give me a hand. I think the Inspector's been hurt."

Brainerd rushed over to the silent figure at the base of the pulpit. "I can't see. Where are the lights?"

Mullen staggered to the door leading out of the auditorium. "There should be a switch. Here it is."

The lights blazed on.

Brainerd looked at Mullen, his shirt was torn and bloodied from a badly cut lip. His left eye was puffed up and there was a large red welt over one cheek bone. Inspector Potter began stirring.

"Don't move, Inspector, it's all over," said Brainerd.

"Did we get him?" Potter propped himself up on one elbow and rubbed the back of his head. The hand came away covered in congealing blood.

Brainerd eased the Inspector to a sitting position and looked at the back of his head. "You're going to have quite a goose-egg. How do you feel?"

Potter tried to get up but sank back. "Like a truck hit me. What about him?"

Brainerd and Mullen looked over at the limp figure stretched out on his stomach.

He was dressed in black pants and turtle-neck sweater. Over his head was a tightly fitting knitted balaclava, similar to those worn by the British Commandos. A narrow eye slit was the only opening. Those for the nose and mouth were sewn up.

"I strongly dislike being jumped in the dark, and I dislike it even more if I don't know who did it. Let's have a look at our friend." Mullen rolled the stirring form over on his back.

Brainerd looked at a large four-cell industrial flashlight lying on the floor. "This is probably what he nailed the Inspector with. Could be the murder weapon."

"Set it up on the platform, Paul. Don't worry about finger prints, he's wearing gloves."

Potter pulled himself up to a sitting position so he could see better.

Mullen licked his lips and looked over at Brainerd. "Well here goes." He pulled the headpiece off and stared in amazement. "It's Steve Gordon!"

Potter sank back to a more comfortable position and murmured, "That figures."

Chapter 17

BRAINERD GAVE THE CRANK one more turn and looked up over the bottom of the bed. "How's that?"

"About half a turn more," replied Ferguson.

"If this doesn't suit you, come around and do it yourself," laughed Brainerd.

"I may just do that. I'm getting sick and tired of being in the hospital anyway. There's nothing wrong with me. I'm going home today regardless of what the doctor says."

"Now stop that, Jimmy," said his wife. "You've only been here just over a day. Behave yourself or I'll ask him to keep you here indefinitely."

Ferguson sat up so Betty could fluff his pillows. "Come on now, Paul, fill me in on what's happened."

"Patience, there's no sense of going over everything twice. Potter and Doug will be here in a few minutes," replied Brainerd.

The door opened and Potter came through, followed by Mullen. The Inspector's head was swathed in bandages and Mullen's face looked raw and sore.

Ferguson laughed. "You two guys look like you've been in a fight."

"Laugh if you want to," said Mullen, as he fingered his swollen eye. "Our wounds came from honorable combat. What have you got to show?"

"A sore stomach. Want to see it?" Ferguson pretended to lift up the covers.

"The party's getting rough, want me to leave?" asked Betty.

"Just boyish enthusiasm, Betty, don't squelch it," admonished Phinnamore from his chair by the window.

"Well, now," said Potter. "Suppose we clean up this entire matter, once and for all. I've a few questions to ask and I'm sure Jimmy's just bursting to know what he missed."

"Bursting is right, Inspector. Suppose you tell me your side of it and I'll fill in mine."

Potter ran a finger under the head bandage. "This is going to drive me right out of my mind. I've never had anything itch so bad in all my life. Let's see, where shall I start?"

Brainerd looked up, "Why not begin from where you and I met in the car?"

"Good idea. You know what happened up to the point of your disappearance, don't you, Jimmy?"

"Yes, that's all clear."

"I met with Paul and instructed him to relieve Doug at the Phinnamore house by five in the afternoon. I had an inkling that everything would start popping about then. Paul went home to warn you about accepting Gordon's invitation, but you had already left." Potter fidgeted in the hard hospital chair.

Phinnamore got up and pushed his chair across the floor. "Here, trade with me, I hate to see an older gentleman in distress."

"I'll settle that older bit with you later. Thanks just the same." Potter moved with obvious difficulty to the more comfortable chair.

He thought for a moment then began. "Paul couldn't wait for you much past four-thirty. Since he was reluctant to upset Betty unduly, he refrained from saying anything other than asking her to have you call me before you made a final decision about the weekend. When Paul called me to say that you hadn't come home I knew things were beginning to move. That's why I had Betty get out of the house and stay with the Phinnamores.

"I was sure that whoever it was would be desperate. We had prodded him into making a move, especially with the picture in the paper. When he called and panicked I felt that it would be wiser to have a younger man like Paul at the church instead of Mr. Phinnamore." Potter nodded in Phinnamore's direction.

131

"I figured you'd get the age bit in somewhere, Inspector," chided Phinnamore.

"That's all right, sir, just want to assure you that I had your best interests in mind at all times." Potter's eyes gleamed.

Mullen saw him fumbling in his pocket. "Here are some matches, Inspector," he said, handing them across the bed.

Ferguson pulled at the bed sheet impatiently while Potter attended to the business of getting his pipe going.

He blew two extended columns of smoke up to the ceiling and said, "Ah, that's more like it." His voice took on an authoritative tone. "I had to assume that the Reverend was being watched so had Paul dress in his suit and leave for the church in his car. Good thing they are about the same size. Once we set everything up in the church it was just a matter of waiting and hoping that the prey would smell the bait. I must say that he was a real scrapper. It's probably a good thing that he put me out of action instead of Doug because I don't think I could have handled him. He had the strength of ten men. Well, that's all there really is to tell about the capture. Suppose you fill me in on what happened after Paul left." Potter looked over at Phinnamore.

Phinnamore didn't answer for a moment, then looked up. "Well, Inspector, we had quite a time. Betty was upset and refused to go to bed. Frankly I didn't blame her. About ten after two or so the telephone rang. Before I could reach it Betty grabbed the receiver. It was Gordon. He disguised his voice and said that Jimmy had just confessed to Scales' murder and was in a rooming house on Bleeker Street. I wanted to call you, but Betty was adamant. She said she was going to Jimmy and would go by herself if I didn't come. I suggested that we try the church first and see if either you or Paul were still there. This satisfied her, and since we didn't have a car we had no other choice but to call a cab. If you've ever tried to get a cab at two-thirty in the morning you'll understand why it was just after three before we got there."

"Good thing, too," mused Mullen. "Any earlier and you could have joined the party."

Brainerd walked to the foot of the bed. "I suppose it's my turn

132

to take over. Betty came bursting into the church with Harrison in her wake. The police had taken Gordon away in a cruiser and the doctor was giving first aid to the Inspector and Doug. They were in no shape to handle things so I decided that there couldn't be too much danger with Gordon out of the way and went with them."

"How did you know where to go?" asked Potter.

"Jimmy had told me that he followed Gordon the other day and saw him enter a large rooming house just around the corner on Bleeker Street. He mentioned that there was a sign in the window when I asked him how he knew it was a rooming house."

"I'll make a detective out of you yet, Paul," replied Potter.

"Thank you, sir. Praise from you is praise well earned."

Potter acknowledged the compliment with a curt nod of his head.

Brainerd continued. "The rest is pretty academic. We found the room, using the process of elimination, broke in and got Jimmy to the hospital as quickly as possible. One thing bothers me though. How come there just happened to be two officers out on the street when we needed them?"

"Simple, my dear fellow, I told them to be there. Each one of you have been covered like a glove for the past week or so." Potter smiled, supremely satisfied.

Brainerd shrugged his shoulders, "That's all for me. You're on, Jimmy."

Ferguson sat straight up in bed. "I suppose that you can call my adventure one of disobedience. If I had listened to Paul and not gone off on my own I wouldn't have gotten into this mess. After the first meeting with Steve I felt sorry for him and really thought he wanted to become friends again. The thought of him being guilty was the farthest thing from my mind. He called in the morning and asked me to meet him in the sporting section of Cannon's Department Store. They were having a special sale on marine hardware and he wanted to pick up some things for the new boat. Since he didn't want to tell Muriel until the boat was bought and in the lake he asked me to help him by keeping quiet. The place was mobbed and when we went to get my car it was boxed in. It was obvious it was useless to try and get it out of the lot. Steve suggested that we take his and pick up mine later so we left it."

"That's where Jimmy's tail lost him. He wasn't expecting another car," said Mullen.

Potter cleared his throat. "Yes, I'll have a word with that officer later about the unexpected. The whole operation could have hinged on that one mistake."

Ferguson looked at the two men and continued. "When we got to the rooming house the fellow who was selling the boat was out. Steve had a key to his room and asked me to wait with him. He hadn't arrived by seven-thirty and Steve was getting mad. He had to go all the way up to the lake for his boat trailer so asked me to wait until he got back. I wanted to go home because I thought Betty would be upset, but he told me not to worry, because he had arranged everything. He said that he'd given Muriel extra money and she was taking Betty out for dinner. Since I'd nothing else to do I agreed. It was after eight and I was starved. Steve said he would send up some Chinese food for me and left. He thought it would take three or four hours before he got back and asked me to wait until at least two. He said it was important for someone to stay otherwise he might lose the boat if the owner came back and no one was there. I thought it was stupid, but said O.K. when he asked it as a special favor because we were friends. After he left I tried to call Betty on the phone in the hall, but there was no answer. I even lost my dime.

"I don't remember much after eating the food. All I know is my stomach is sure sore from all the tubes and probing. What was in that food—rat poison?"

"Not quite, but something nearly as lethal. He slipped you about thirty Nembutal capsules broken open and all mixed up in the food. You had enough sleeping compound to put you out until the second coming," answered Potter.

"Perhaps I can fill in some loose pieces now. Gordon was no rank amateur. He was a cunning professional blackmailer turned homicidal."

Betty gasped, "You're not serious?"

"Never been more serious, my dear. He had about half a dozen that we know about on the go. There could be more. It all started about ten years ago when Gordon was committed to Twin Acres suffering from a severe mental breakdown. He was so bad in fact that his chances of ever being released were pretty slim. Somehow, through self-determination and the use of drugs he made a remarkable recovery. During his rehabilitation he worked as a clerk in the administration office at Twin Acres. He became so efficient that he was given the run of the place and trusted implicitly. His finances were at a low ebb, so he devised a devilish plan. Every chance he got, he studied the files of current and past patients. By eliminating those without money or position he built up a file of prospective marks. One, for example, is a highly successful doctor who did time for performing an abortion on a young girl who died. He suffered a complete breakdown and spent most of his term in Twin Acres. Upon his release, he changed his name, re-entered university and graduated as a dentist. Today he is a highly successful orthodontist who has been paying Gordon regularly. Gordon threatened to expose him to the medical college if he didn't come through."

"How awful!" exclaimed Betty. "How could he have done such a thing?"

"Quite simple, Betty. He should never have been released. He was not cured, just an excellent actor. The one thing that he hadn't planned on was Charlie Scales. When he heard you and Jimmy were coming to Fairview he thought it would be fun to drive you up the wall with fake telephone calls. Some people get their kicks from drugs or liquor, Gordon got his from mysterious telephone calls. In some cases he got quite obscene from what we've learned since his capture."

"What about Muriel?" asked Ferguson. "Did she know all this was going on?"

"Not really. He met her at Twin Acres where she was a ward aide. Muriel idolizes her husband and was content to go along with whatever he says, no questions asked."

"What will become of her?" asked Betty.

"I really don't know. She's one of those pathetic by-products of

135

a situation such as this. It's hard to say. Reverend Phinnamore is the one to be thanked for bringing this to a head. When he got fed up and intimated that he would turn the tapes over to us regardless of the consequences Gordon panicked. He couldn't touch Mr. Phinnamore without revealing his identity so he did the next best thing. He tried to scare him. That's why he wrecked the office. Charlie Scales was just an unfortunate victim of circumstances. He was driving by, and like the good council member he was, made it a point to check the church for any open windows or lights which may have been left on. He must have seen the beam from Gordon's flashlight and decided to investigate. Since he had a key he had no problem getting into the building quietly. When he surprised Gordon as he was wrecking the office Gordon was forced to silence him. Scales ran into the choir room to hide, but was found and you know the rest."

"Why didn't he run right out into the street?" asked Phinnamore.

"You'd think he would, but it's hard to say. Probably he was scared out of his wits, to say nothing of being shocked at seeing Gordon doing such a thing. People do funny things when they are terrified. After he killed Scales there was nothing else for him to do but bluff his way through. He had made a point of joining in at Fairview and establishing a perfect cover. He was sure the police would be looking for a prowler. He watched the church and when he saw Mr. Phinnamore and Jimmy go in he wanted to find out how much they knew. That's why he called just as you left. He had to be sure whether or not you two had found Scales' body."

Potter indicated to Mullen that he wanted a drink of water. After he had taken a couple of long draughts and relit his pipe he continued. "Jimmy's attitude following his arrest and appearance at the inquest gave Gordon the perfect out. He wanted to bring Jimmy to the point of nervous collapse and cash in on his irrational thinking."

"I could see this building up in Jimmy and since I didn't have a better idea I decided to help the situation along. I didn't know about Gordon and really didn't suspect him until later. I knew that Jimmy was innocent so asked him to co-operate. I figured I'd better bring Betty into it so I asked her to help him have a nervous breakdown or appear to have one. You carried your part off very well, my boy." Potter leaned forward and slapped Ferguson's leg.

"Who said I was acting? If you really want to know I was just about two steps away from the animal farm," replied Ferguson.

"Everything was just going fine until you disappeared, Jimmy. That kinda threw me. Since I had no idea where you were I had to rely on my instinct. I couldn't imagine Gordon doing away with you without first leading us on a merry chase. You were the perfect fall guy. It was established that you were suspect in the eyes of the police and he needed you to get him off the hook. When we captured him and Paul lit out after you I felt that everything was going to work out just fine. I didn't consider the overdose of sleeping capsules, however. That was a nice touch by Gordon. It gave him the perfect opportunity to have you leave a suicide note in your own handwriting, shaky though it might be. It pinned everything on you. His hospital background became useful. He knew from experience that it took about half an hour for the Nembutal to take effect. It was tasteless and you would never notice it in the food, especially Chinese food."

"What did he put it in?" asked Ferguson.

"The sweet and sour breaded shrimps."

"My favorite, I always clean up the plate including the sauce."

"He was sure you would. Why do you think he made a point of becoming close friends? He wanted to know you as well as you know yourself. All this information was filed in the back of his mind for future reference. That bit came in handy as you can see."

"Whose room was it, Inspector?" asked Phinnamore. "Did he have an accomplice?"

"No, there never was anyone else. He rented the room under a different name so he could have somewhere to keep his records. He never did anything from home."

"I find that hard to believe, Inspector, the working alone bit."

"Why's that, Jimmy?"

"Well, when I met Steve at the restaurant, that first time, I'm sure his car was parked in the lot. But when we came out it was gone."

"No mystery, Jimmy, he probably had Muriel pick it up. That would give him the excuse for you to drive him to the rooming house. He wanted you to accept him being there. It also permitted Muriel to see that he was trying to patch things up."

"Well, I suppose so. It all sounds like Greek to me," replied Ferguson.

"I'm just guessing about the car bit, but I'll check it out when I question Gordon again if you like."

"O.K., I'd like to know. Funny how a stupid thing like that bugs you."

"Not at all. It's simple things like that which have solved hopeless cases. Right, Paul?"

"You bet, Inspector. One thing I'd like to know."

"What's that?" asked Potter.

"How come he came in the front way when he specifically asked for the back door to be left open?"

Potter smiled, "Simple, he's as smart as they come. He had a front door key he'd managed to steal and kept it for just such an emergency. He'd no more intention of being surprised than we had."

Potter looked around the room at each face. "Any further questions?"

"Yes," asked Betty. "What will happen to Steve?"

"It's not up to me, Betty, it's up to the courts. He appeared this morning and was remanded for psychiatric examination pending the setting of a trial date. It's my guess that he'll never be brought before a jury. They'll probably declare him unfit to stand trial and recommend a committal to an institution for the criminally insane."

"Does that mean he'll never get out?"

"Not necessarily, Betty. If he's committed it'll be at the pleasure of Her Majesty. That means his case will be reviewed from time to time. If he is ever judged to be sane again he could be released, but it will be a long time. His chances are better than they would have been years ago because of the new techniques and drugs the psychiatrists have to use."

Phinnamore stood up and rubbed his back. "I don't know about the rest of you, but I've got an old-fashioned camp meeting coming

138

up in a few days and I've got work to do."

"Right you are," said Brainerd. "Seems to me I'm involved somehow. Wait for me."

Ferguson yelled, "What am I supposed to do, twiddle my thumbs?"

The telephone rang, breaking into his objection. Everyone stopped and looked at it. It rang again, and again.

"Well, aren't you going to answer it?" asked Phinnamore.

"I'm never going to answer the telephone again," replied Ferguson.

Betty picked up the receiver. "Hello. Yes, I'll tell him. Thank you."

"Well?"

"Well what, honey?"

"Who was it?"

"You aren't interested in telephone calls so why should I tell you? It was only the ward supervisor calling to say that Dr. Williams has signed your discharge and you can go home."

"Oh!" Ferguson sat back in bed. "*Oh!* Give me five minutes and I'll be right with you. Betty, get my pants!"

It was a beautiful Sunday morning. The sun was shining and the birds singing. The tent was practically filled to its utmost capacity and the ushers were busily placing extra chairs at the rear. The side flap opened and leading the platform party was the minister of Fairview Community Church, Harrison Phinnamore, followed by the newly appointed associate minister and director of youth, James Ferguson, and, bringing up the rear, the evangelist, Paul Brainerd.

Standing at the rear just inside the back flap were Inspector Potter and Sergeant Mullen.

"We'll begin the service by singing hymn number sixty-five," announced Phinnamore.

"Well, Doug, I guess we'd better get back to work. What do you say?"

The two men turned, and as they walked down the street to their car the air was filled by a grateful congregation singing "To God be the glory, great things He hath done. . . ."